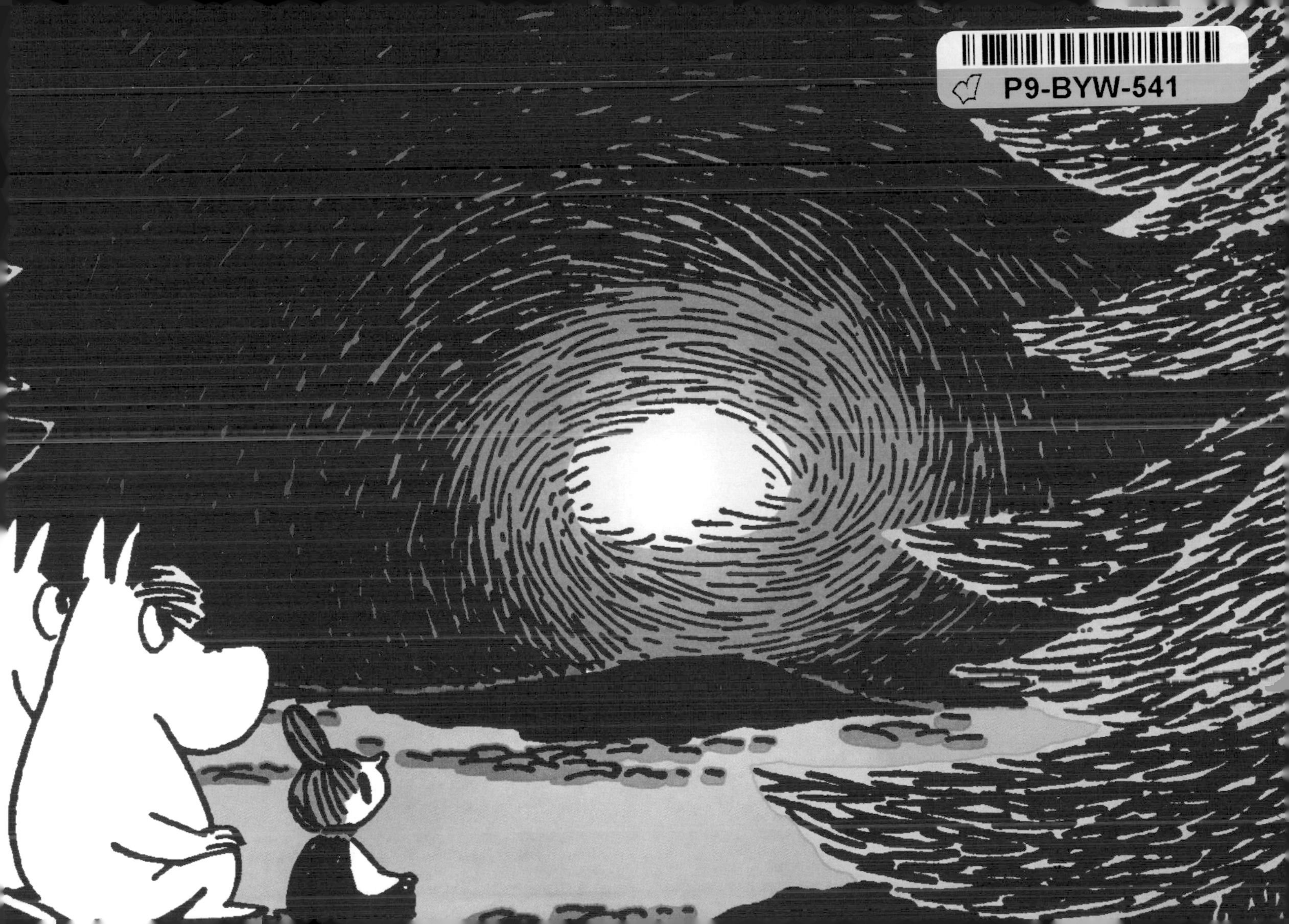

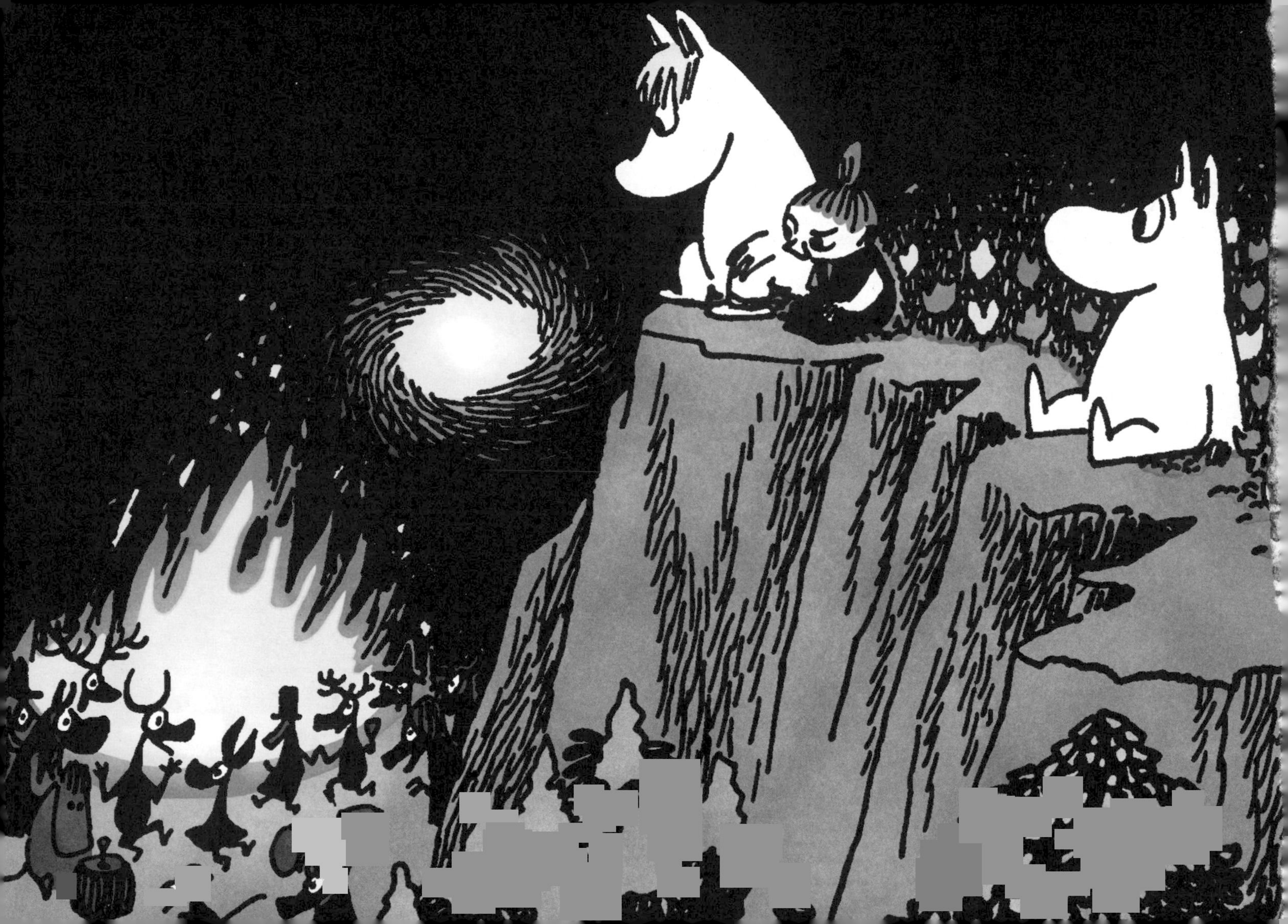

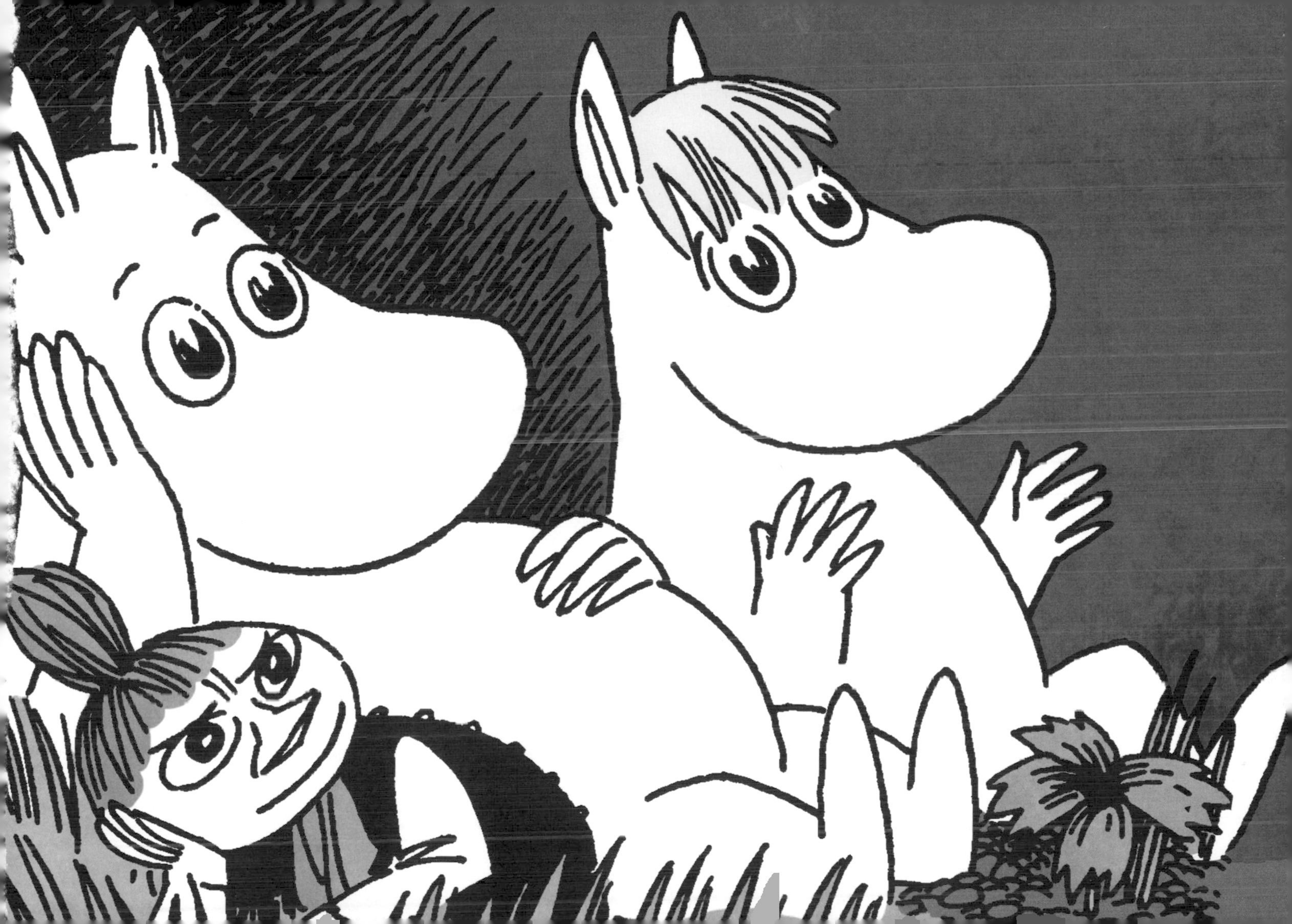

Entire contents © copyright 2013 by Solo/Bulls.
All rights reserved. No part of this book (except
small portions for review purposes) may be
reproduced in any form without written
permission from Solo/Bulls or Enfant.

Moomin and the Comet is written by Lars Jansson
and drawn by Tove Jansson.

Enfant is an imprint of Drawn & Quarterly.

www.drawnandquarterly.com

First edition: July 2013
Printed in Malaysia
10 9 8 7 6 5 4 3 2 1

Library and Archives Canada Cataloguing in Publication
Jansson, Tove
Moomin and the Comet / Tove Jansson.
ISBN 978-1-77046-122-2
1. Graphic novels. I. Title.
PZ7.7.J35M24 2013   j741.5'94897
    C2012-907127-7

Published in the USA by Enfant, a client publisher of
Farrar, Straus and Giroux
18 West 18th Street
New York, NY 10011
Orders: 888.330.8477

Published in Canada by Enfant, a client publisher of
Raincoast Books
2440 Viking Way
Richmond, BC V6V 1N2
Orders: 800.663.5714

Distributed in the United Kingdom by
Publishers Group UK
63-66 Hatton Garden
London
EC1N 8LE
info@pguk.co.uk

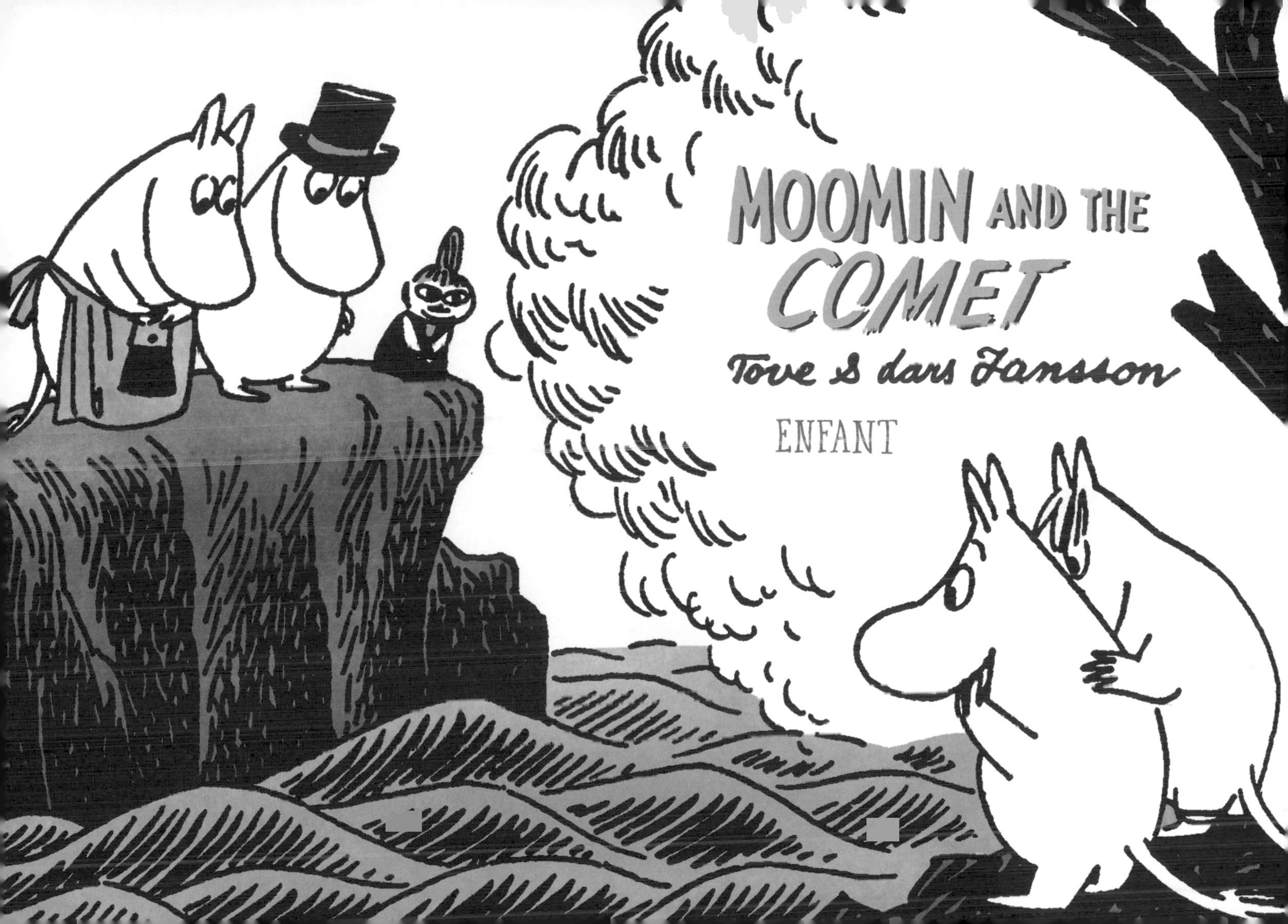
MOOMIN AND THE COMET
Tove & Lars Jansson
ENFANT

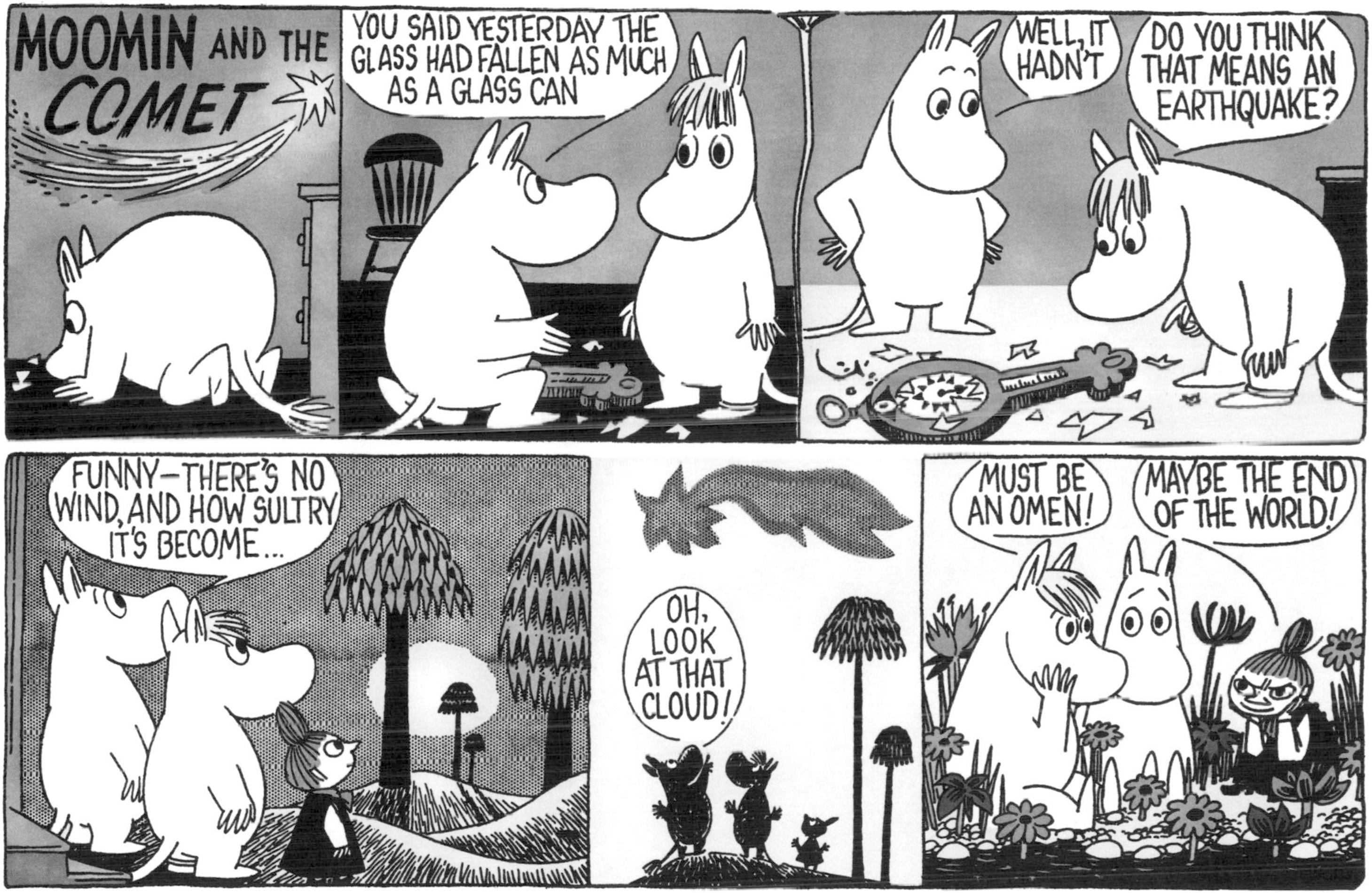
MOOMIN AND THE COMET
YOU SAID YESTERDAY THE GLASS HAD FALLEN AS MUCH AS A GLASS CAN
WELL, IT HADN'T
DO YOU THINK THAT MEANS AN EARTHQUAKE?
FUNNY—THERE'S NO WIND, AND HOW SULTRY IT'S BECOME...
OH, LOOK AT THAT CLOUD!
MUST BE AN OMEN!
MAYBE THE END OF THE WORLD!

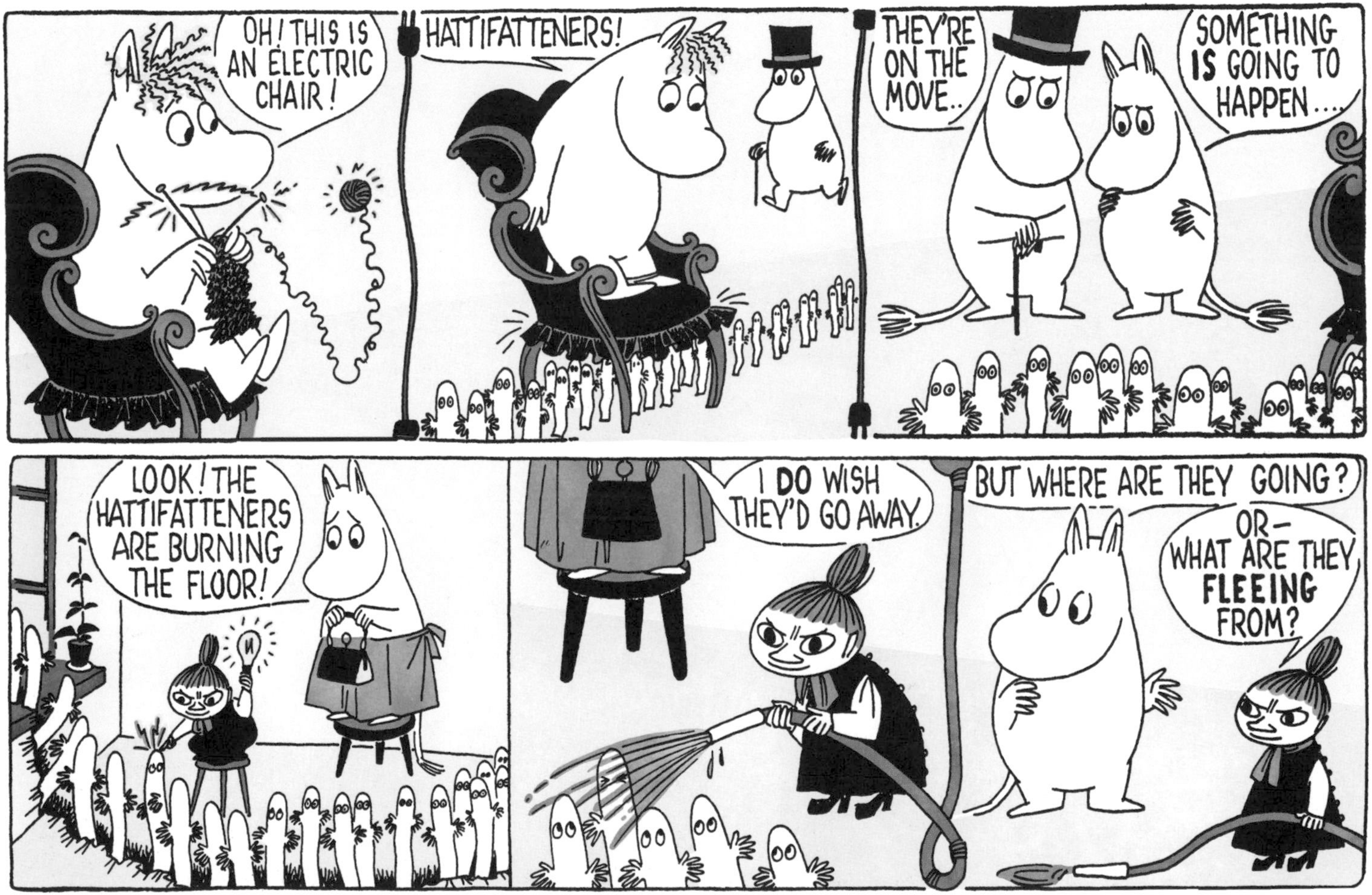
OH! THIS IS AN ELECTRIC CHAIR!
HATTIFATTENERS!
THEY'RE ON THE MOVE..
SOMETHING IS GOING TO HAPPEN....
LOOK! THE HATTIFATTENERS ARE BURNING THE FLOOR!
I DO WISH THEY'D GO AWAY.
BUT WHERE ARE THEY GOING?
OR– WHAT ARE THEY FLEEING FROM?

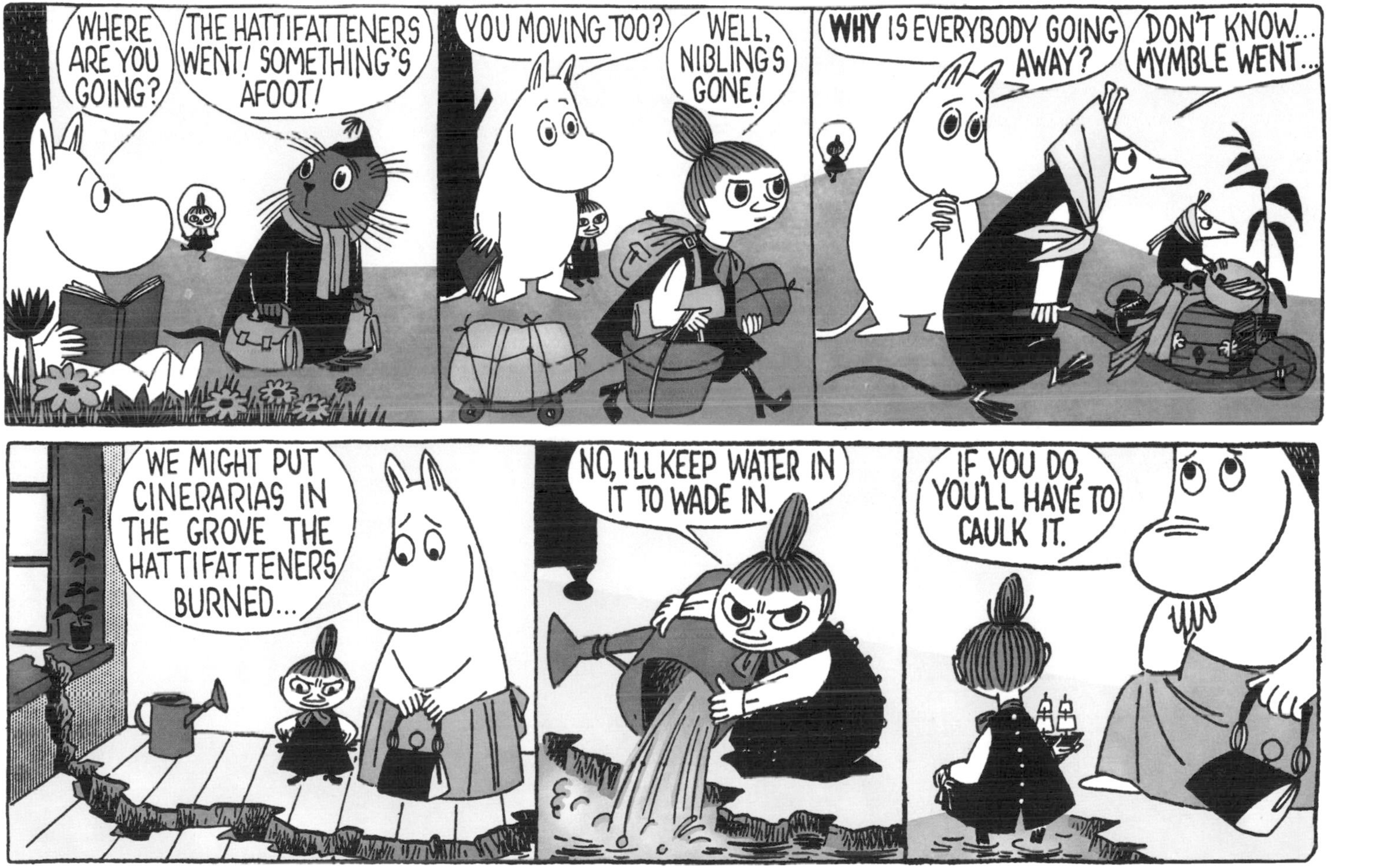
WHERE ARE YOU GOING?
THE HATTIFATTENERS WENT! SOMETHING'S AFOOT!
YOU MOVING TOO?
WELL, NIBLINGS GONE!
WHY IS EVERYBODY GOING AWAY?
DON'T KNOW... MYMBLE WENT...
WE MIGHT PUT CINERARIAS IN THE GROVE THE HATTIFATTENERS BURNED...
NO, I'LL KEEP WATER IN IT TO WADE IN.
IF YOU DO, YOU'LL HAVE TO CAULK IT.

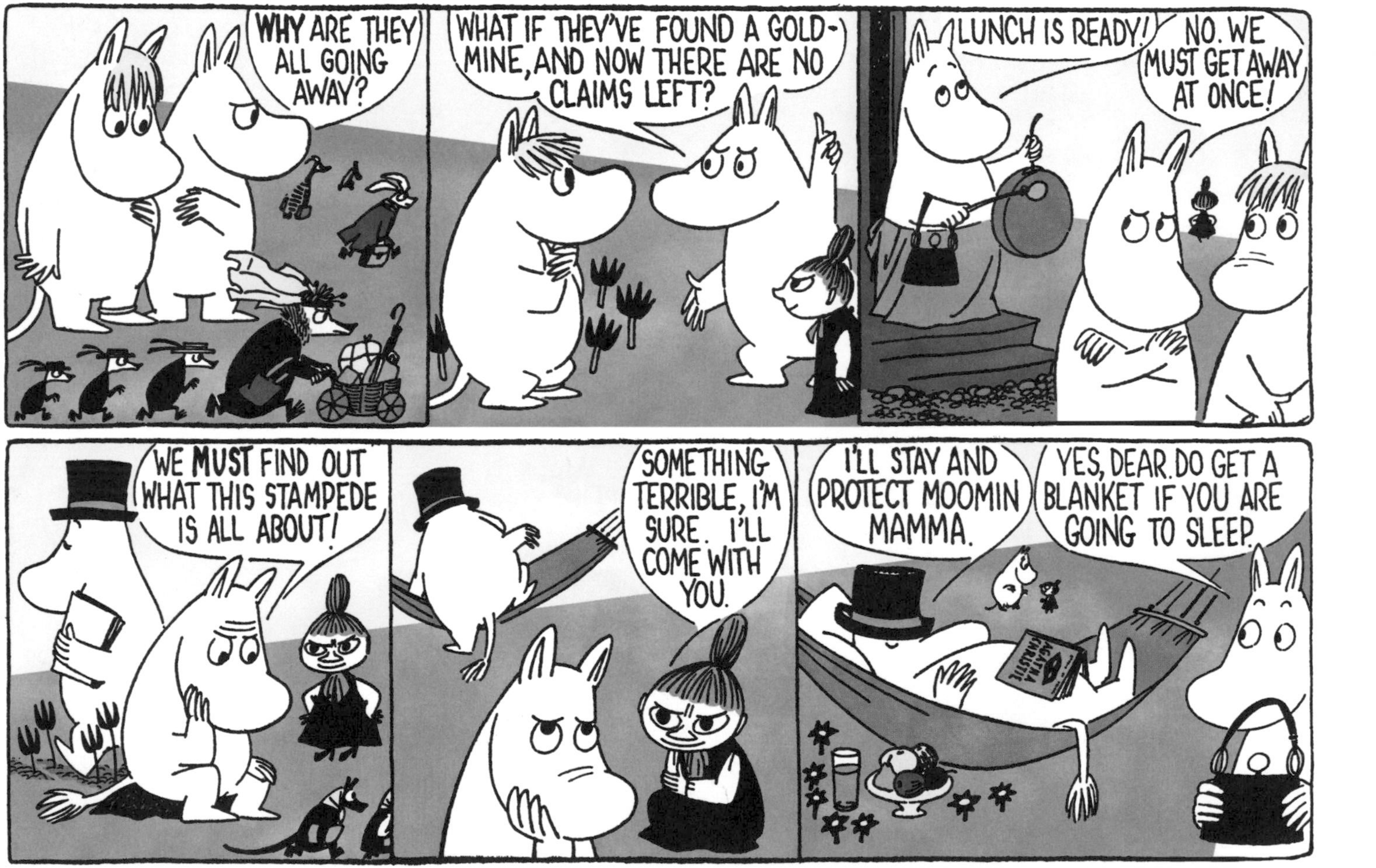
WHY ARE THEY ALL GOING AWAY?
WHAT IF THEY'VE FOUND A GOLD-MINE, AND NOW THERE ARE NO CLAIMS LEFT?
LUNCH IS READY!
NO. WE MUST GET AWAY AT ONCE!
WE MUST FIND OUT WHAT THIS STAMPEDE IS ALL ABOUT!
SOMETHING TERRIBLE, I'M SURE. I'LL COME WITH YOU.
I'LL STAY AND PROTECT MOOMIN MAMMA.
YES, DEAR. DO GET A BLANKET IF YOU ARE GOING TO SLEEP.
AGATHA CHRISTIE

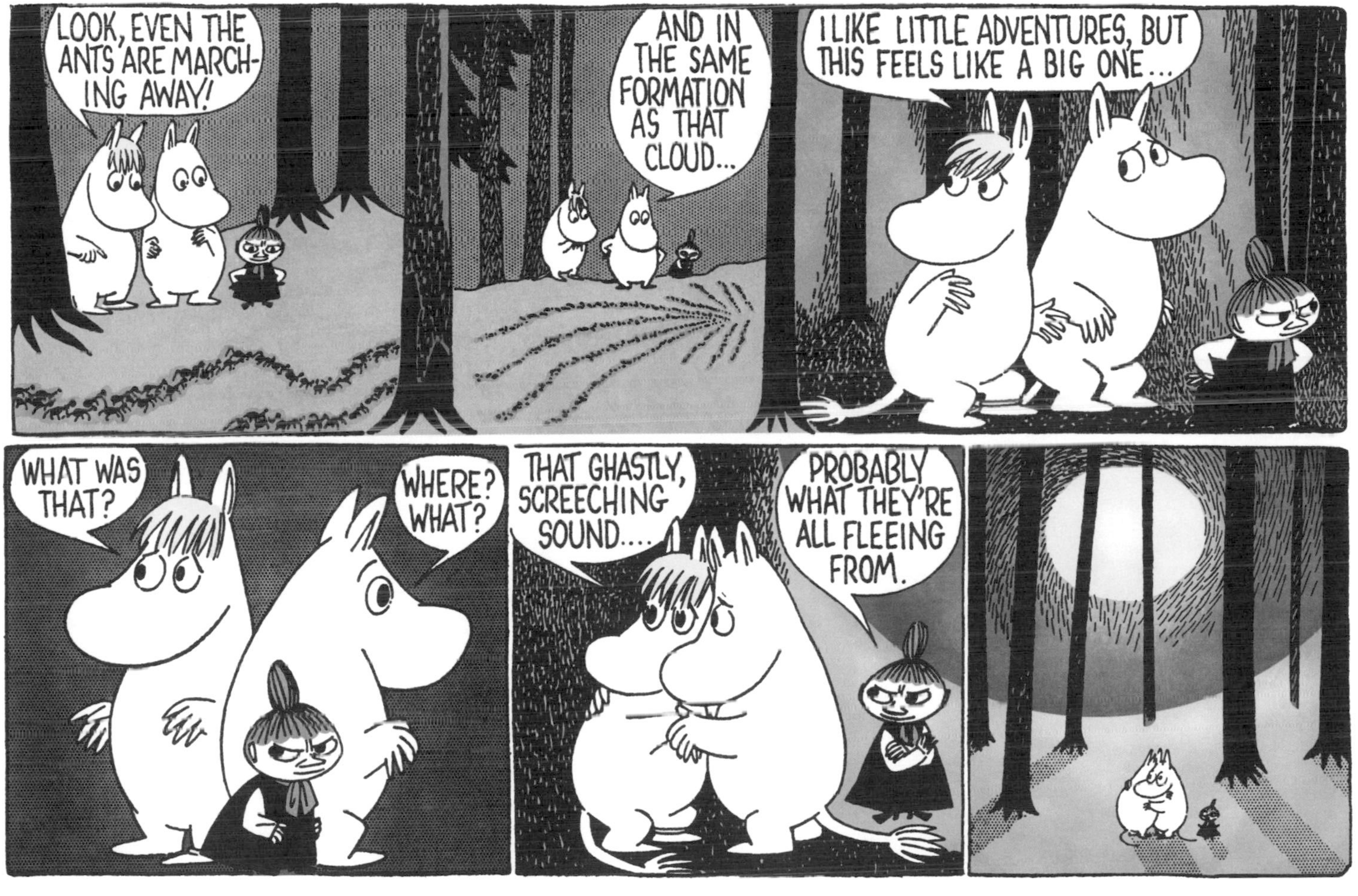
LOOK, EVEN THE ANTS ARE MARCHING AWAY!
AND IN THE SAME FORMATION AS THAT CLOUD...
I LIKE LITTLE ADVENTURES, BUT THIS FEELS LIKE A BIG ONE...
WHAT WAS THAT?
WHERE? WHAT?
THAT GHASTLY, SCREECHING SOUND....
PROBABLY WHAT THEY'RE ALL FLEEING FROM.

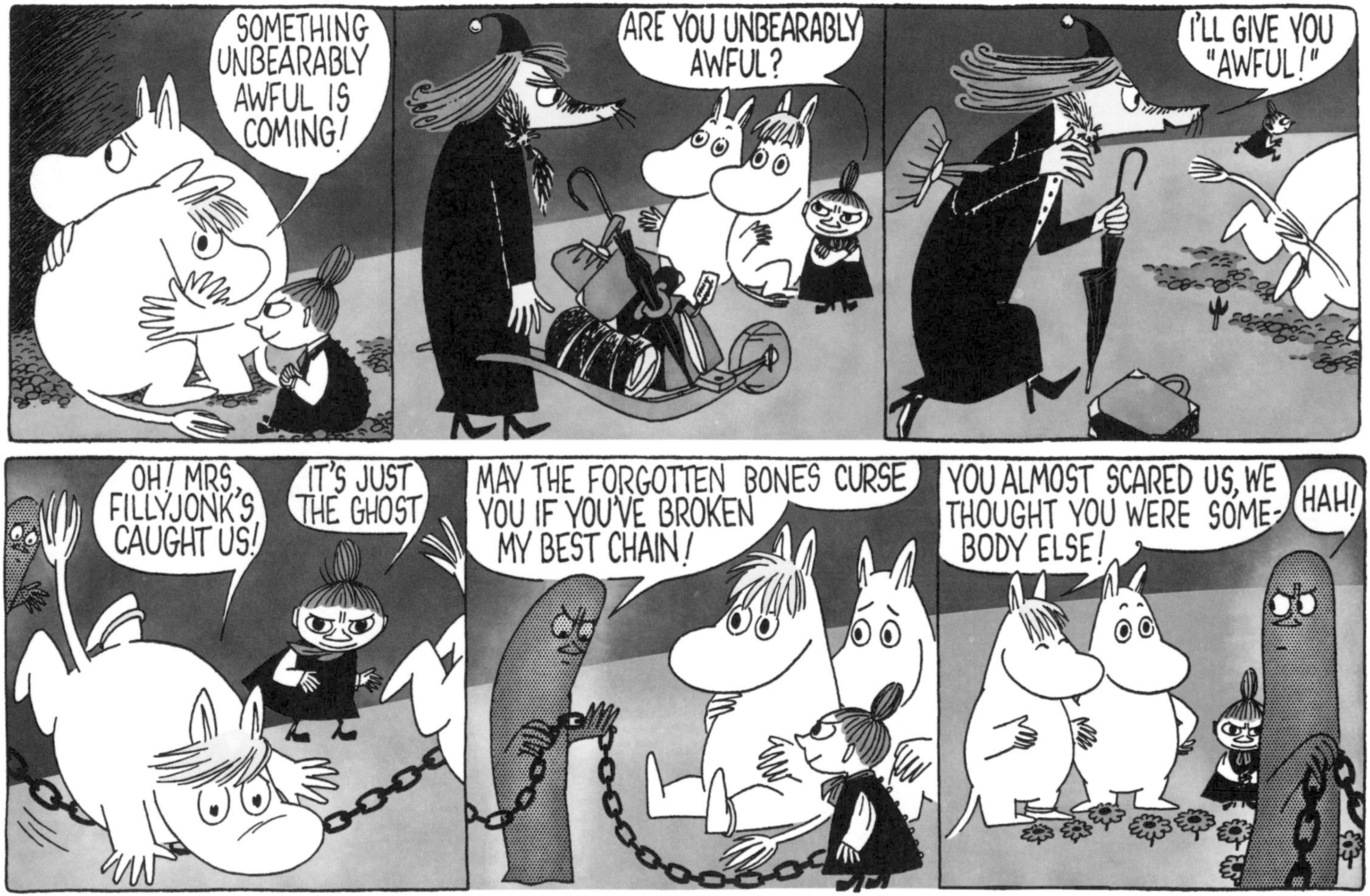
SOMETHING UNBEARABLY AWFUL IS COMING!
ARE YOU UNBEARABLY AWFUL?
I'LL GIVE YOU "AWFUL!"
OH! MRS FILLYJONK'S CAUGHT US!
IT'S JUST THE GHOST
MAY THE FORGOTTEN BONES CURSE YOU IF YOU'VE BROKEN MY BEST CHAIN!
YOU ALMOST SCARED US, WE THOUGHT YOU WERE SOME-BODY ELSE!
HAH!

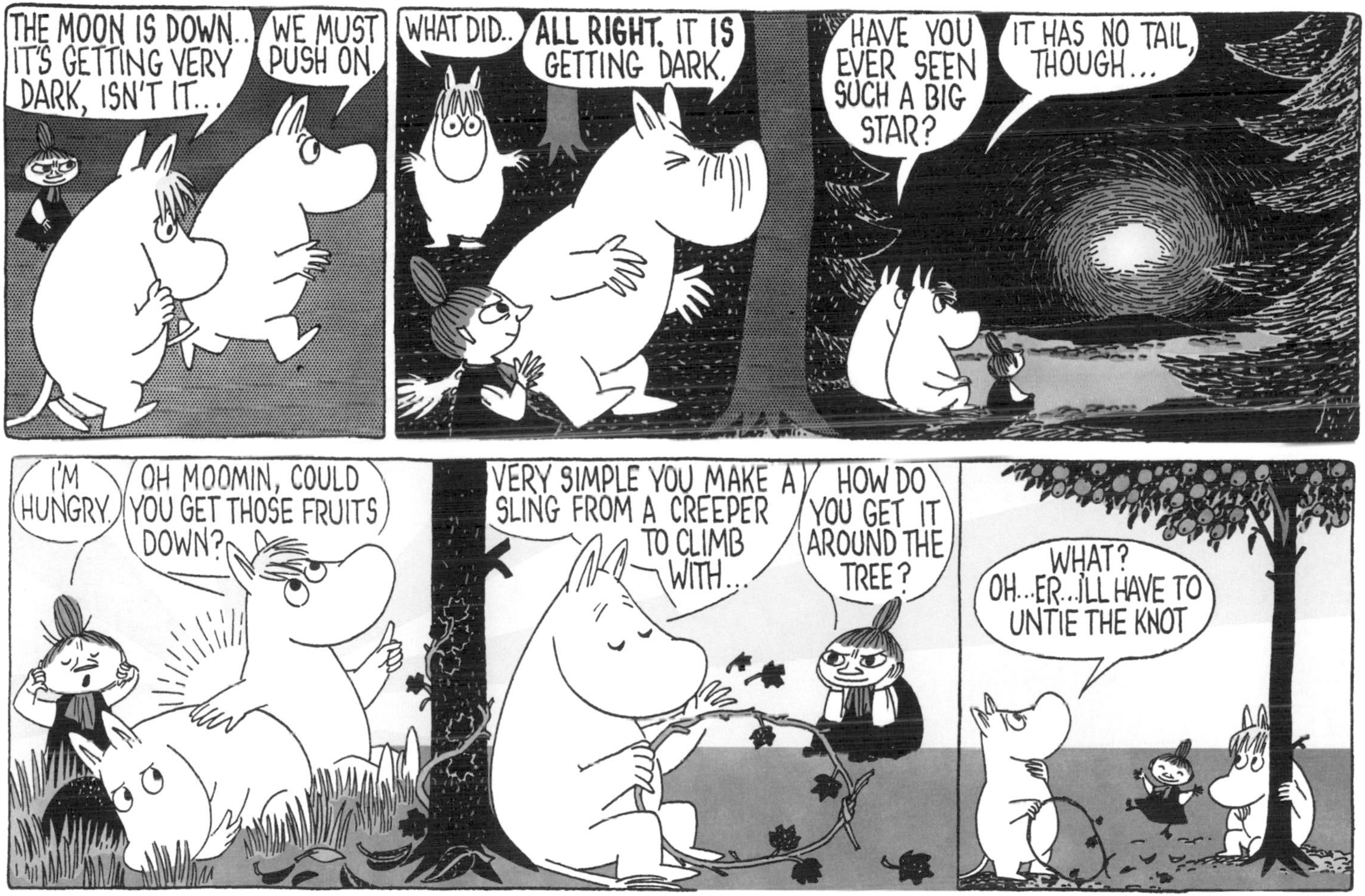
THE MOON IS DOWN.. IT'S GETTING VERY DARK, ISN'T IT...
WE MUST PUSH ON.
WHAT DID..
ALL RIGHT, IT IS GETTING DARK.
HAVE YOU EVER SEEN SUCH A BIG STAR?
IT HAS NO TAIL, THOUGH...
I'M HUNGRY.
OH MOOMIN, COULD YOU GET THOSE FRUITS DOWN?
VERY SIMPLE YOU MAKE A SLING FROM A CREEPER TO CLIMB WITH...
HOW DO YOU GET IT AROUND THE TREE?
WHAT? OH...ER...I'LL HAVE TO UNTIE THE KNOT

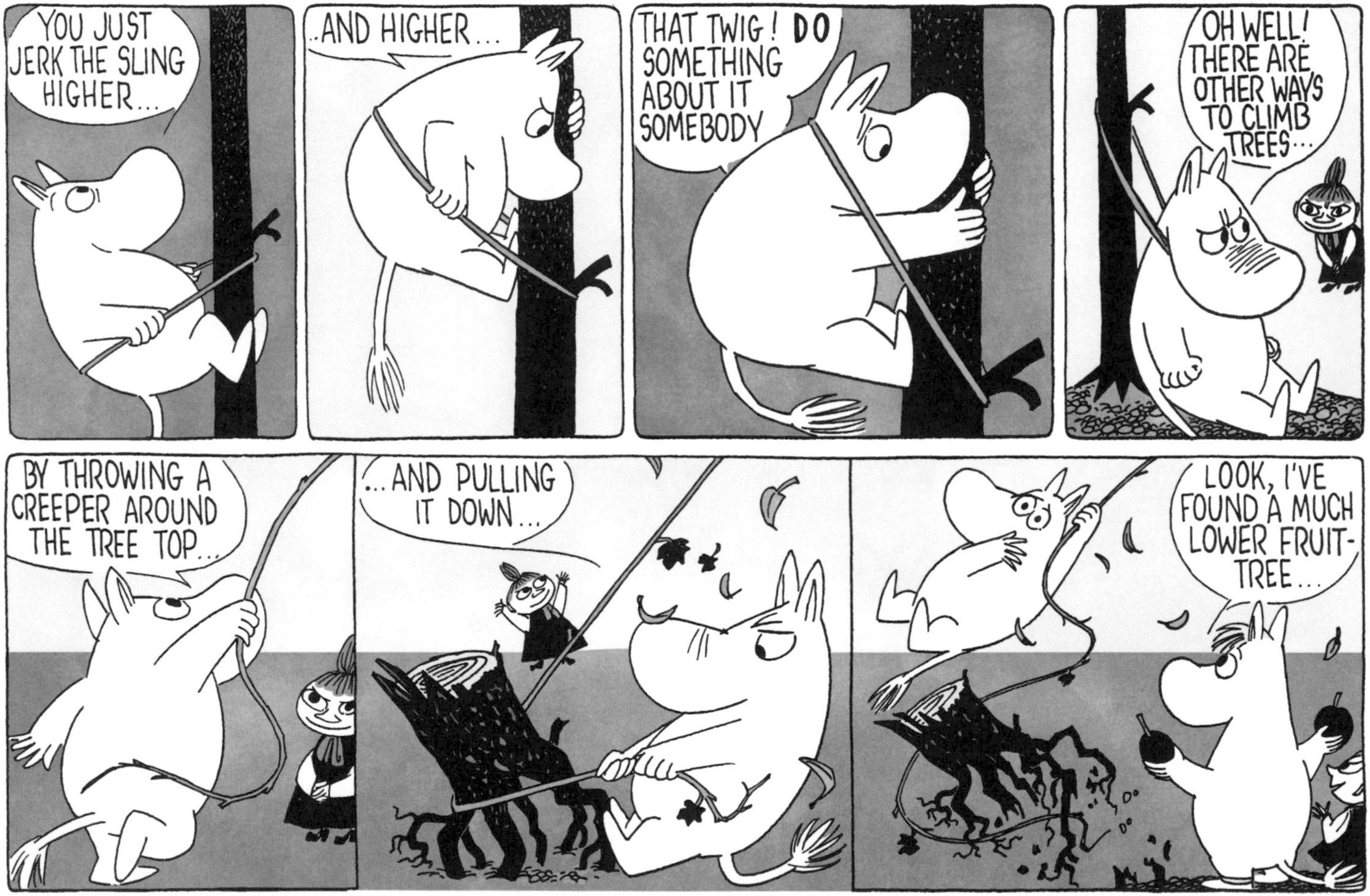
YOU JUST JERK THE SLING HIGHER...
..AND HIGHER...
THAT TWIG! DO SOMETHING ABOUT IT SOMEBODY
OH WELL! THERE ARE OTHER WAYS TO CLIMB TREES...
BY THROWING A CREEPER AROUND THE TREE TOP...
...AND PULLING IT DOWN...
LOOK, I'VE FOUND A MUCH LOWER FRUIT-TREE...

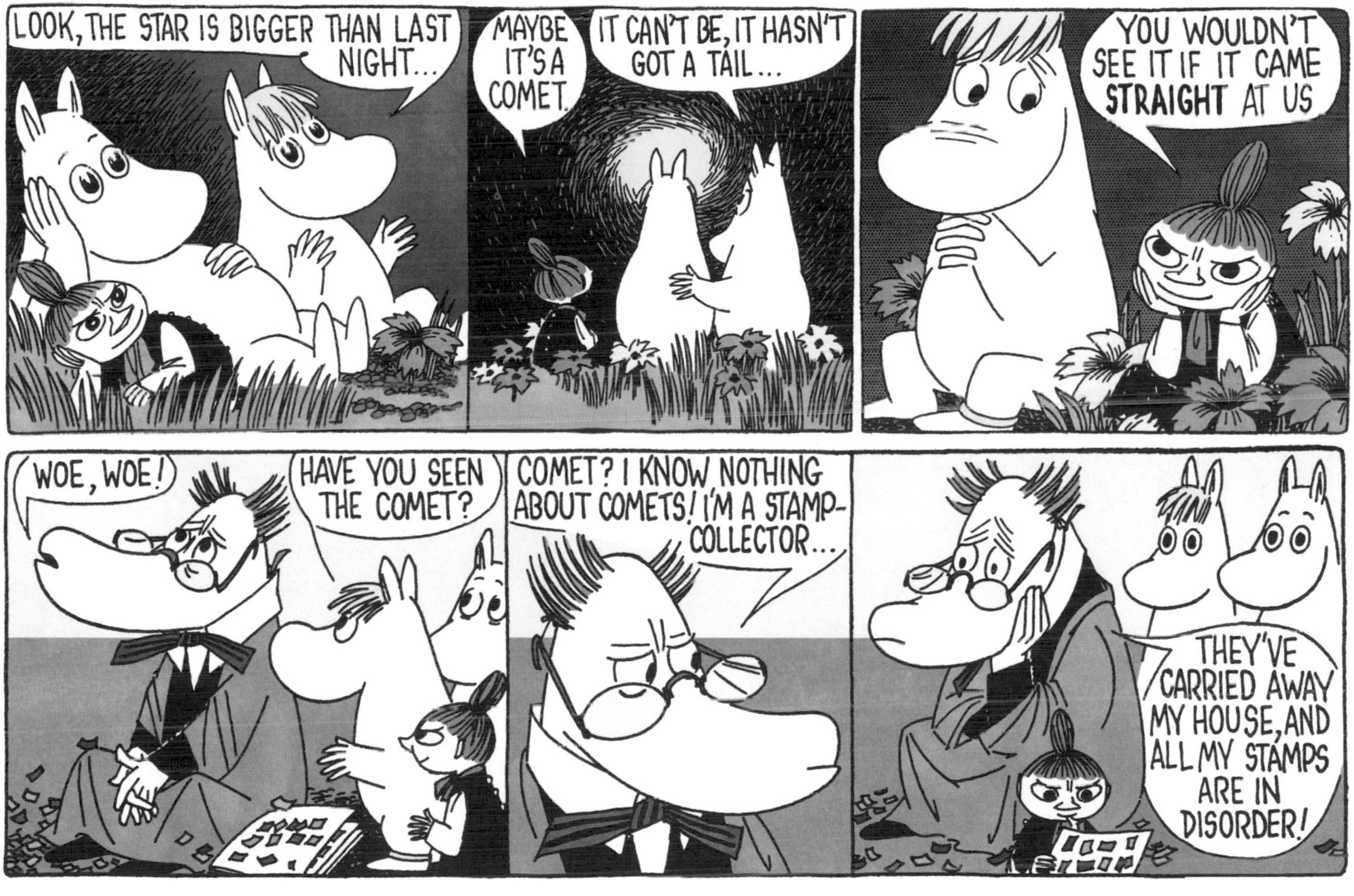
LOOK, THE STAR IS BIGGER THAN LAST NIGHT...
MAYBE IT'S A COMET.
IT CAN'T BE, IT HASN'T GOT A TAIL...
YOU WOULDN'T SEE IT IF IT CAME STRAIGHT AT US
WOE, WOE!
HAVE YOU SEEN THE COMET?
COMET? I KNOW NOTHING ABOUT COMETS! I'M A STAMP-COLLECTOR...
THEY'VE CARRIED AWAY MY HOUSE, AND ALL MY STAMPS ARE IN DISORDER!

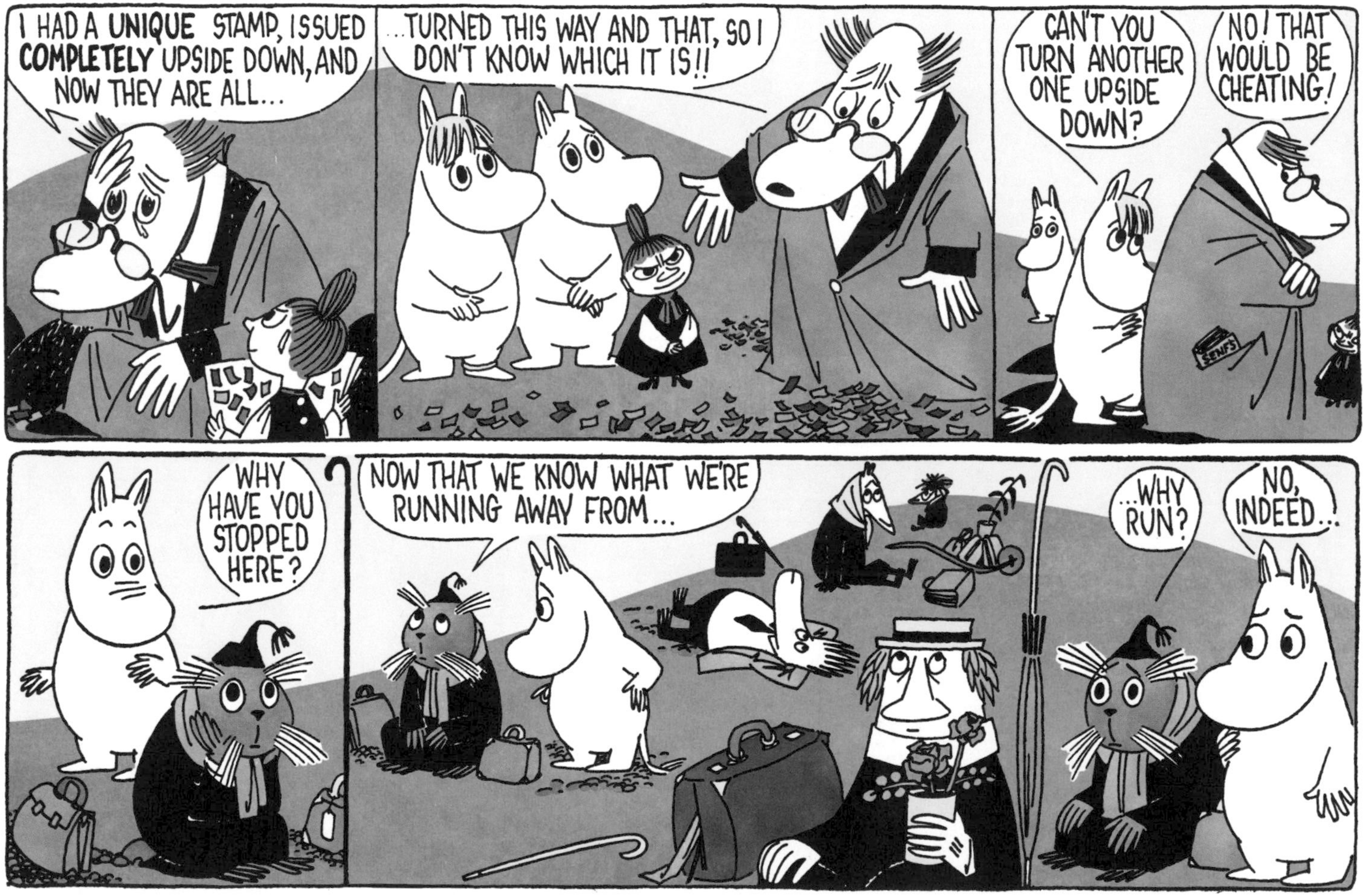
I HAD A **UNIQUE** STAMP, ISSUED **COMPLETELY** UPSIDE DOWN, AND NOW THEY ARE ALL...
...TURNED THIS WAY AND THAT, SO I DON'T KNOW WHICH IT IS!!
CAN'T YOU TURN ANOTHER ONE UPSIDE DOWN?
NO! THAT WOULD BE CHEATING!
SENFS
WHY HAVE YOU STOPPED HERE?
NOW THAT WE KNOW WHAT WE'RE RUNNING AWAY FROM...
...WHY RUN?
NO, INDEED...

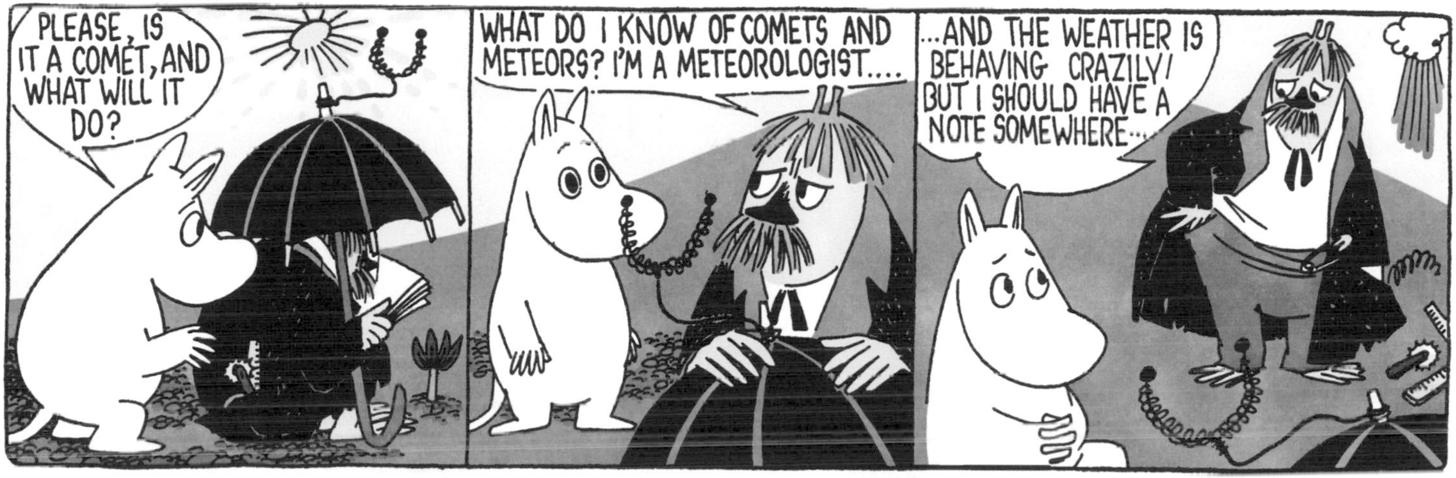
PLEASE, IS IT A COMET, AND WHAT WILL IT DO?
WHAT DO I KNOW OF COMETS AND METEORS? I'M A METEOROLOGIST....
...AND THE WEATHER IS BEHAVING CRAZILY! BUT I SHOULD HAVE A NOTE SOMEWHERE...

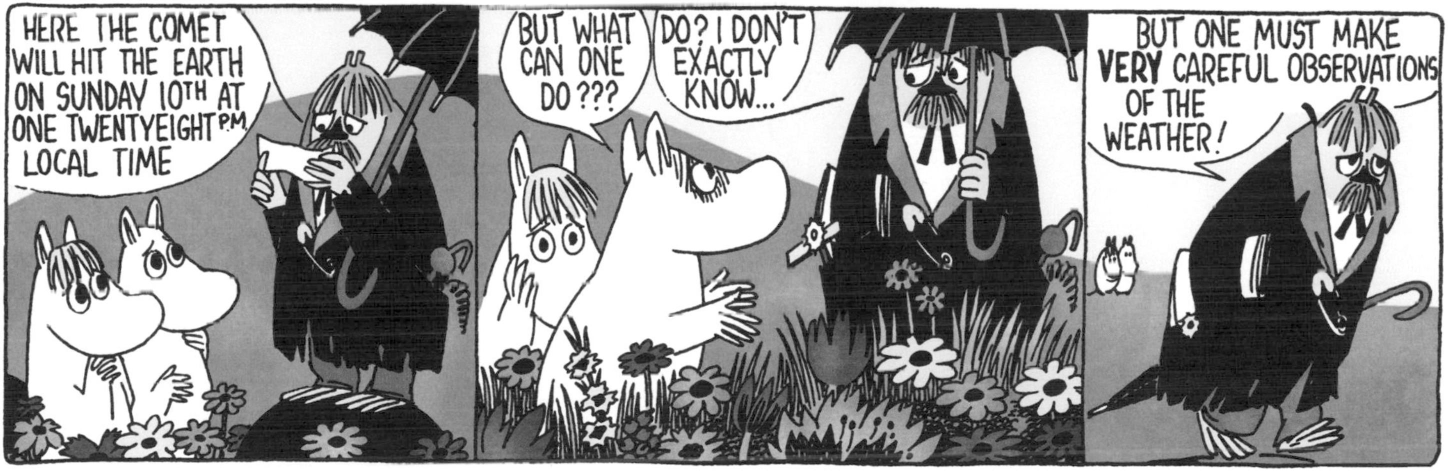
HERE THE COMET WILL HIT THE EARTH ON SUNDAY 10TH AT ONE TWENTYEIGHT P.M. LOCAL TIME
BUT WHAT CAN ONE DO???
DO? I DON'T EXACTLY KNOW...
BUT ONE MUST MAKE VERY CAREFUL OBSERVATIONS OF THE WEATHER!

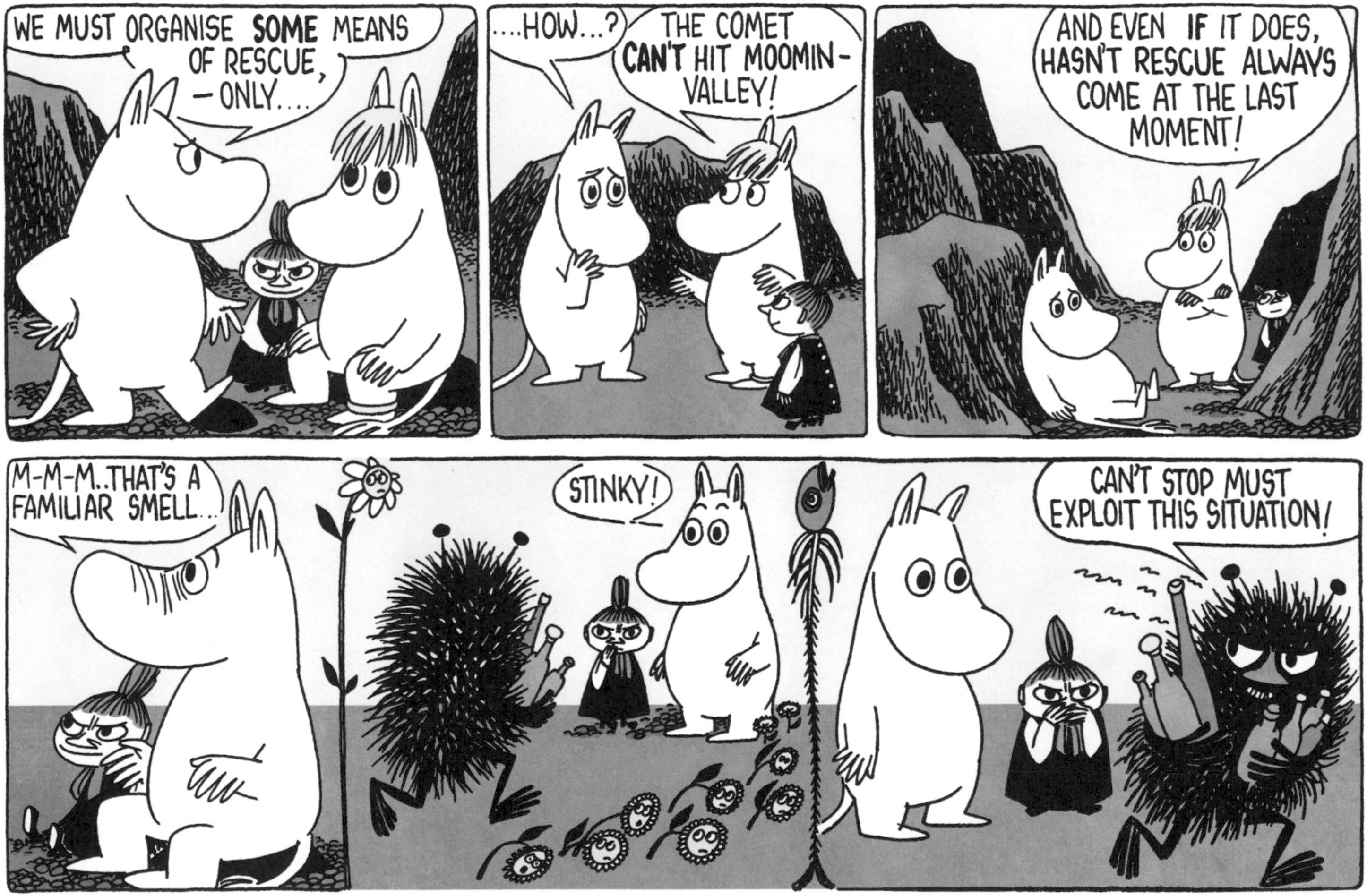
WE MUST ORGANISE **SOME** MEANS OF RESCUE, — ONLY....
....HOW...?
THE COMET **CAN'T** HIT MOOMIN-VALLEY!
AND EVEN **IF** IT DOES, HASN'T RESCUE ALWAYS COME AT THE LAST MOMENT!
M-M-M..THAT'S A FAMILIAR SMELL...
STINKY!
CAN'T STOP MUST EXPLOIT THIS SITUATION!

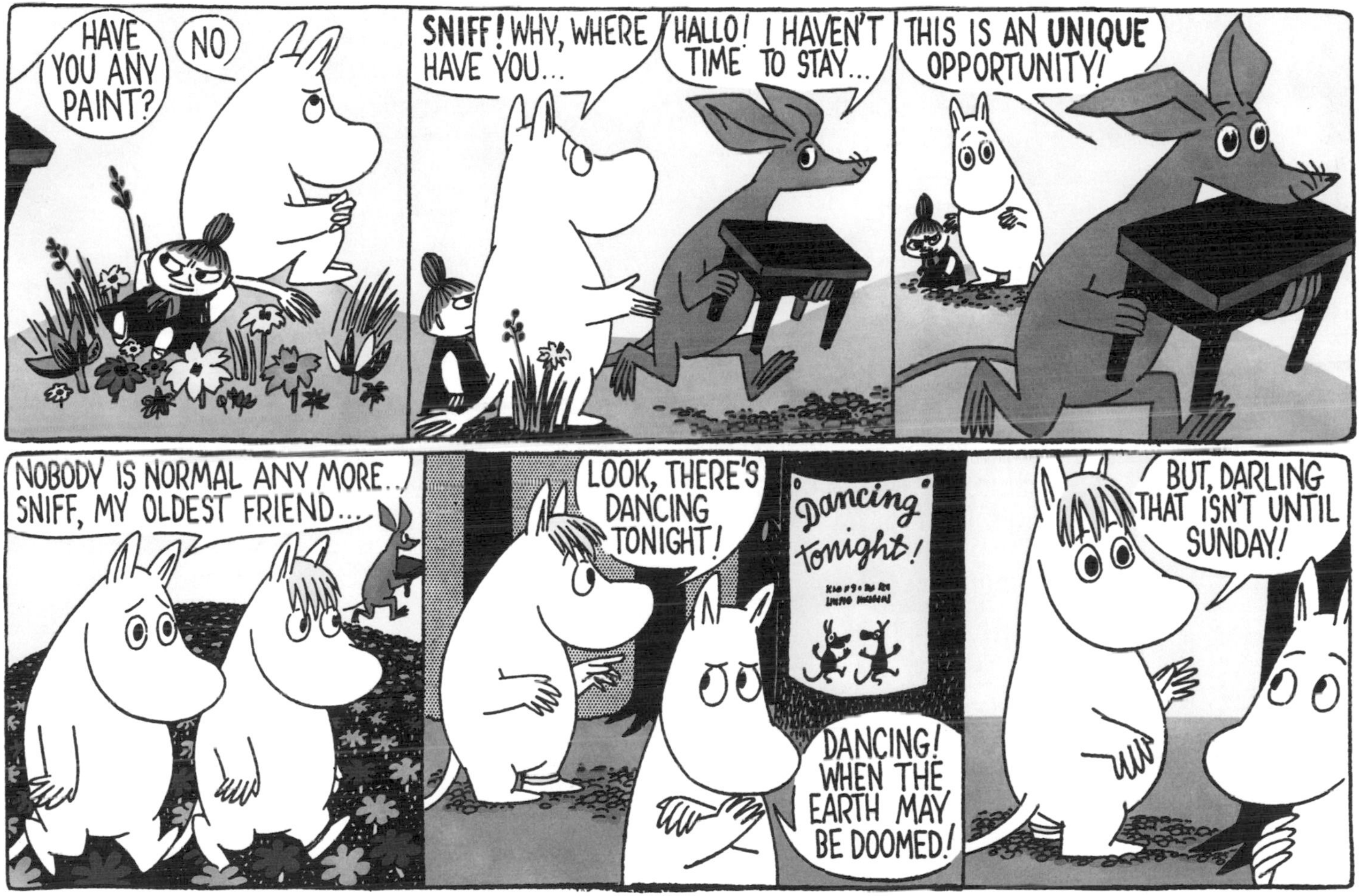
HAVE YOU ANY PAINT?
NO
SNIFF! WHY, WHERE HAVE YOU...
HALLO! I HAVEN'T TIME TO STAY...
THIS IS AN UNIQUE OPPORTUNITY!
NOBODY IS NORMAL ANY MORE.. SNIFF, MY OLDEST FRIEND...
LOOK, THERE'S DANCING TONIGHT!
Dancing Tonight!
DANCING! WHEN THE EARTH MAY BE DOOMED!
BUT, DARLING THAT ISN'T UNTIL SUNDAY!

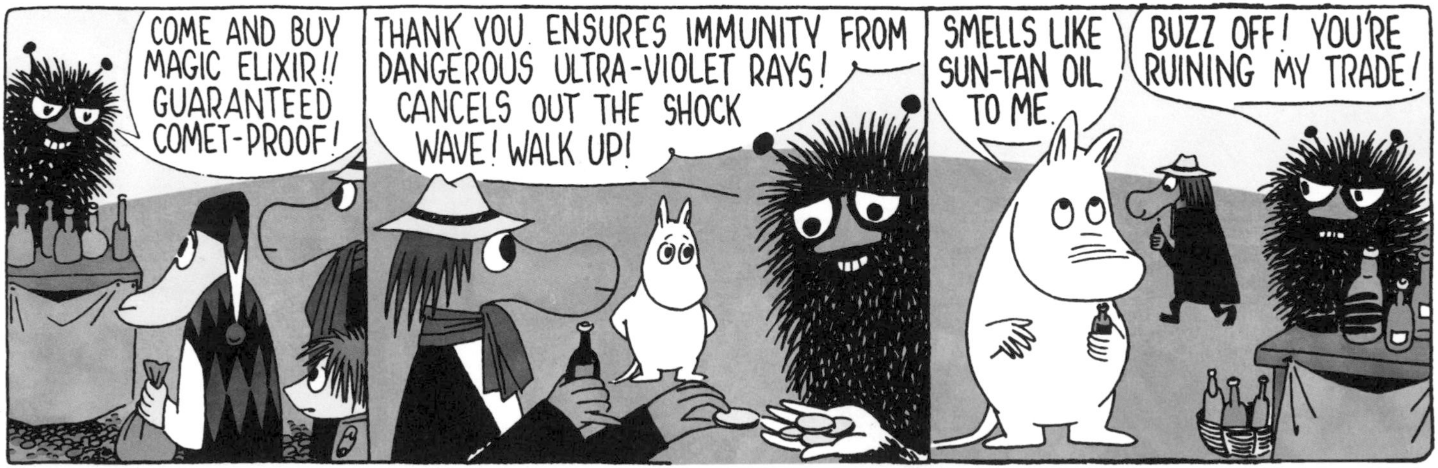
COME AND BUY MAGIC ELIXIR!! GUARANTEED COMET-PROOF!
THANK YOU. ENSURES IMMUNITY FROM DANGEROUS ULTRA-VIOLET RAYS! CANCELS OUT THE SHOCK WAVE! WALK UP!
SMELLS LIKE SUN-TAN OIL TO ME.
BUZZ OFF! YOU'RE RUINING MY TRADE!

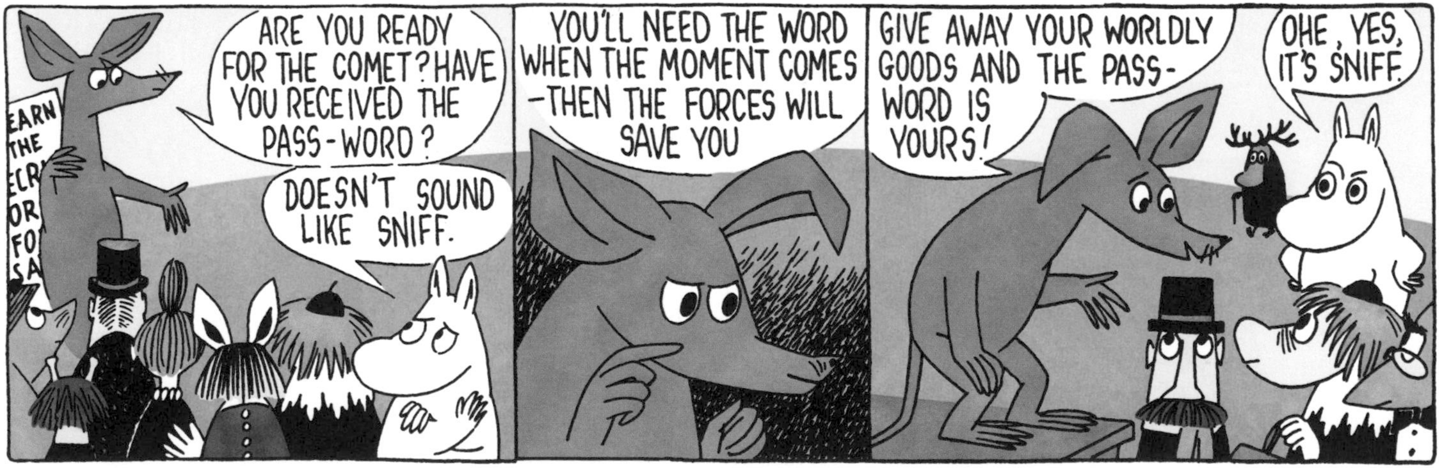
ARE YOU READY FOR THE COMET? HAVE YOU RECEIVED THE PASS-WORD?
DOESN'T SOUND LIKE SNIFF.
YOU'LL NEED THE WORD WHEN THE MOMENT COMES -THEN THE FORCES WILL SAVE YOU
GIVE AWAY YOUR WORLDLY GOODS AND THE PASS-WORD IS YOURS!
OHE, YES, IT'S SNIFF.

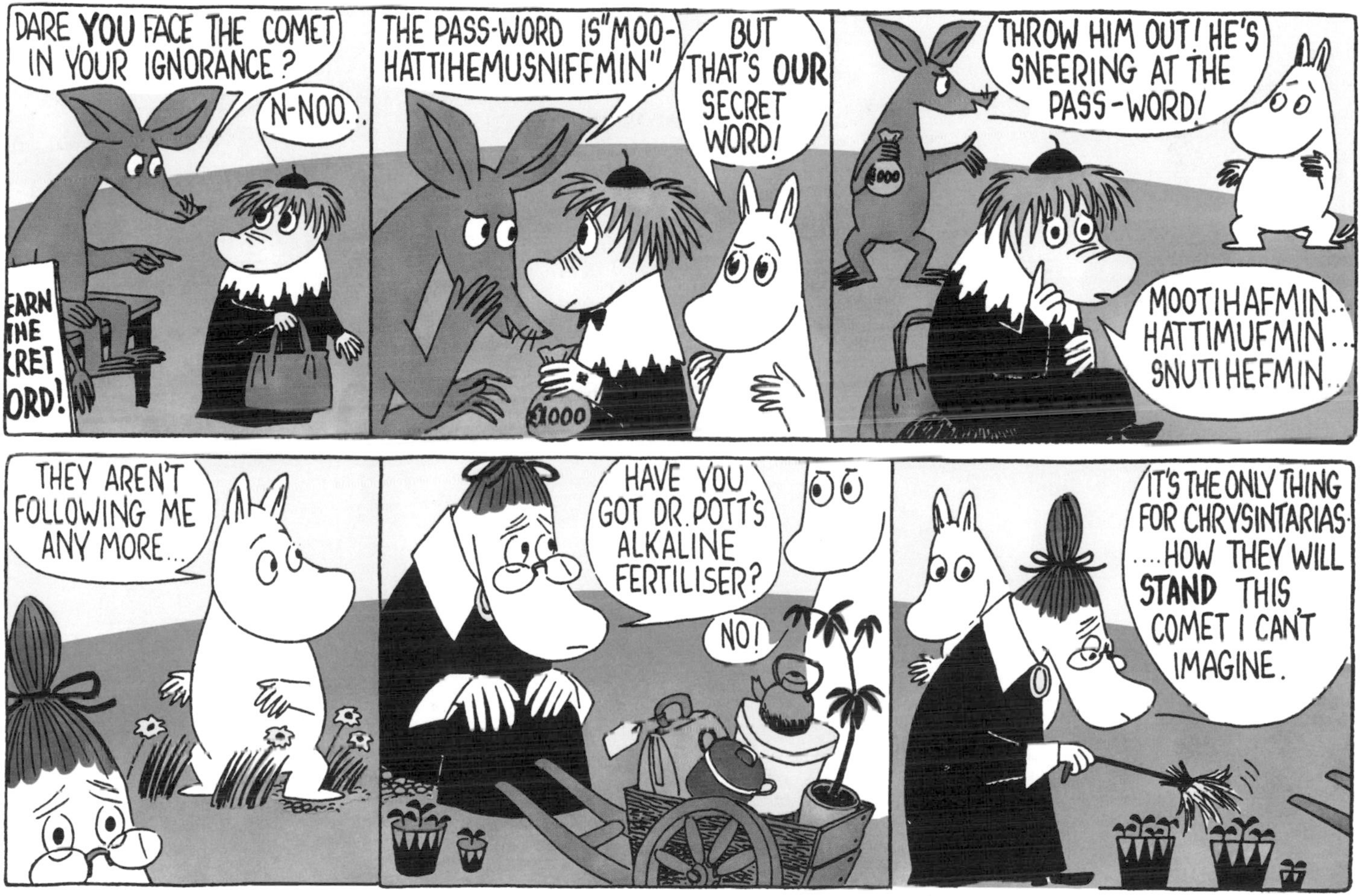
DARE YOU FACE THE COMET IN YOUR IGNORANCE?
N-NOO...
EARN THE CRET ORD!
THE PASS-WORD IS "MOO-HATTIHEMUSNIFFMIN".
BUT THAT'S OUR SECRET WORD!
£1000
THROW HIM OUT! HE'S SNEERING AT THE PASS-WORD!
MOOTIHAFMIN... HATTIMUFMIN... SNUTIHEFMIN...
THEY AREN'T FOLLOWING ME ANY MORE...
HAVE YOU GOT DR. POTT'S ALKALINE FERTILISER?
NO!
IT'S THE ONLY THING FOR CHRYSINTARIAS. ...HOW THEY WILL STAND THIS COMET I CAN'T IMAGINE.

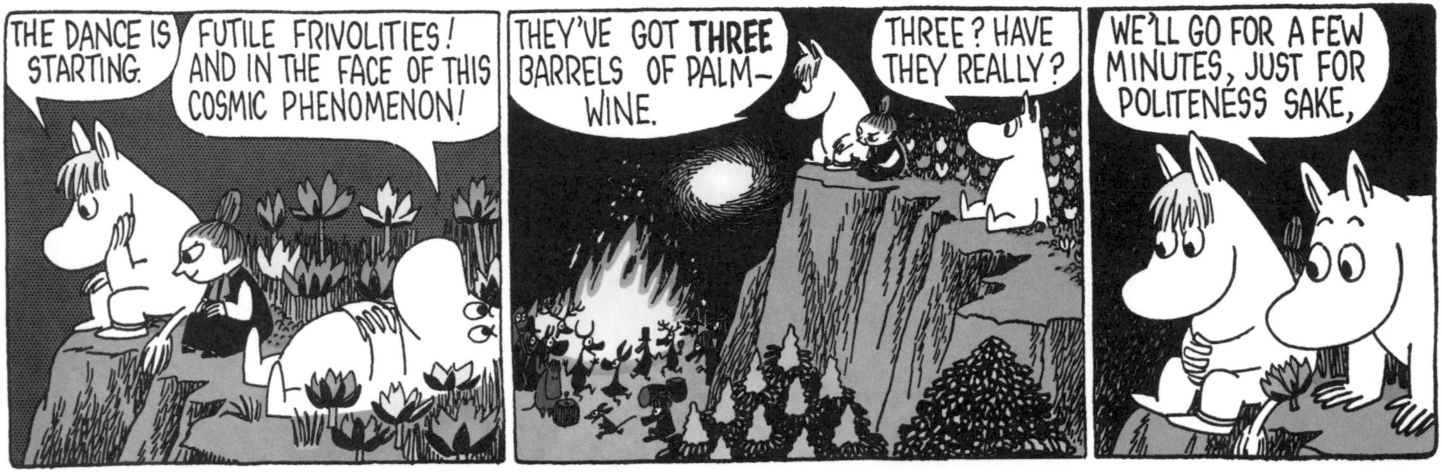
THE DANCE IS STARTING.
FUTILE FRIVOLITIES! AND IN THE FACE OF THIS COSMIC PHENOMENON!
THEY'VE GOT **THREE** BARRELS OF PALM-WINE.
THREE? HAVE THEY REALLY?
WE'LL GO FOR A FEW MINUTES, JUST FOR POLITENESS SAKE,

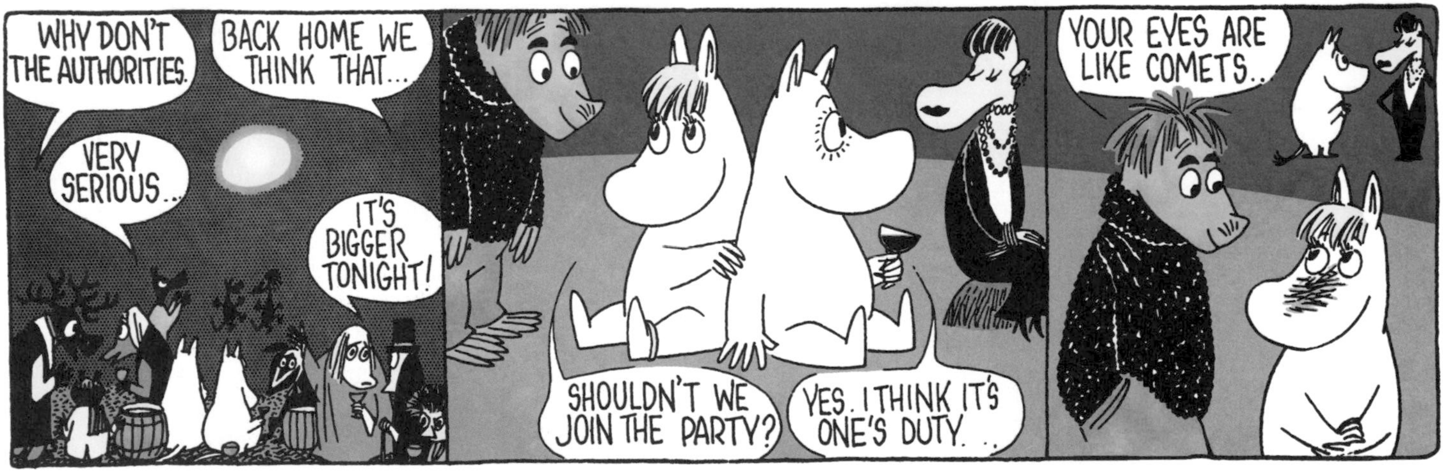
WHY DON'T THE AUTHORITIES.
BACK HOME WE THINK THAT...
VERY SERIOUS...
IT'S BIGGER TONIGHT!
SHOULDN'T WE JOIN THE PARTY?
YES. I THINK IT'S ONE'S DUTY. . .
YOUR EYES ARE LIKE COMETS..

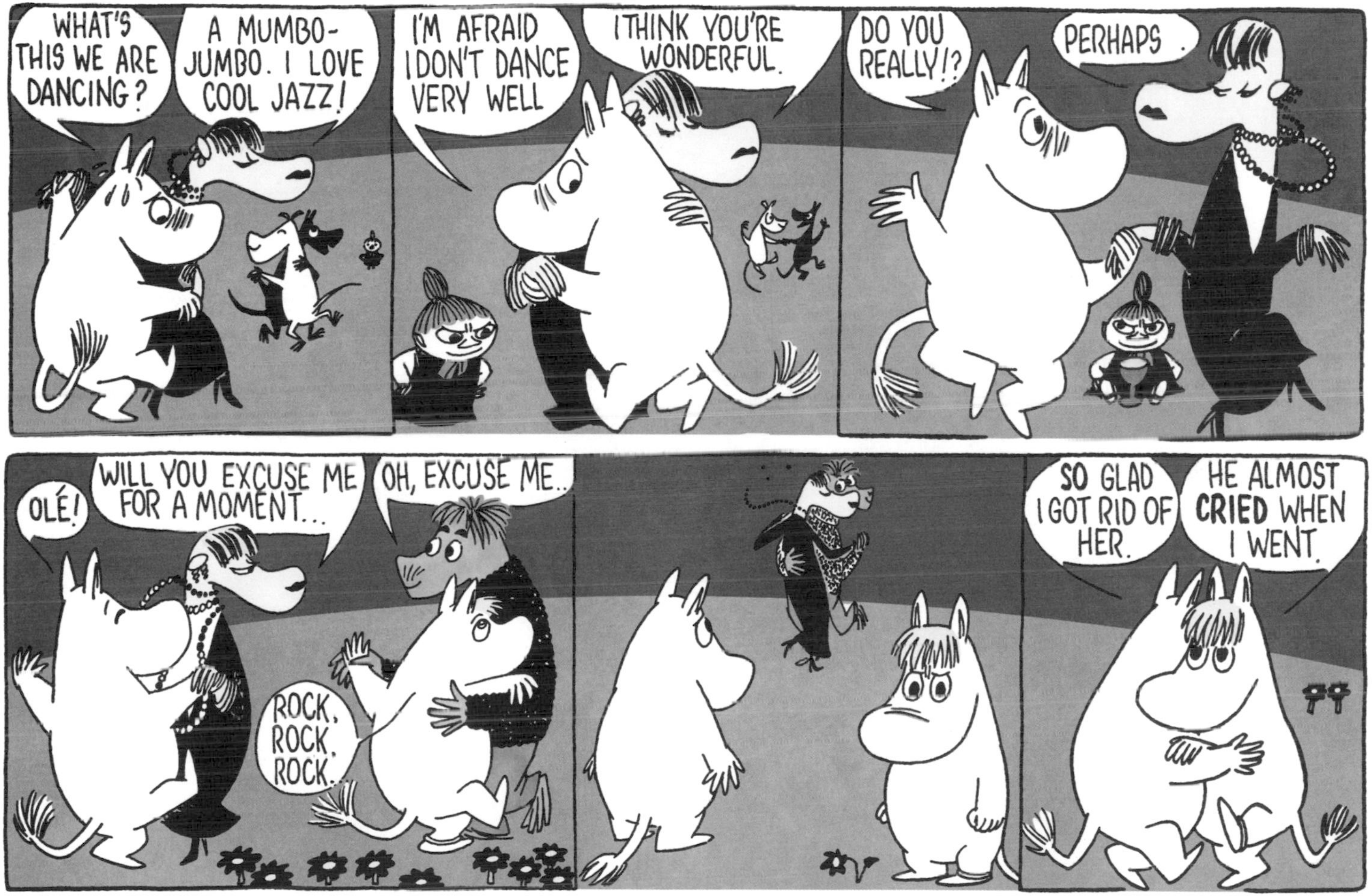
WHAT'S THIS WE ARE DANCING?
A MUMBO-JUMBO. I LOVE COOL JAZZ!
I'M AFRAID I DON'T DANCE VERY WELL
I THINK YOU'RE WONDERFUL.
DO YOU REALLY!?
PERHAPS.
OLÉ!
WILL YOU EXCUSE ME FOR A MOMENT...
OH, EXCUSE ME..
ROCK, ROCK, ROCK.
SO GLAD I GOT RID OF HER.
HE ALMOST CRIED WHEN I WENT.

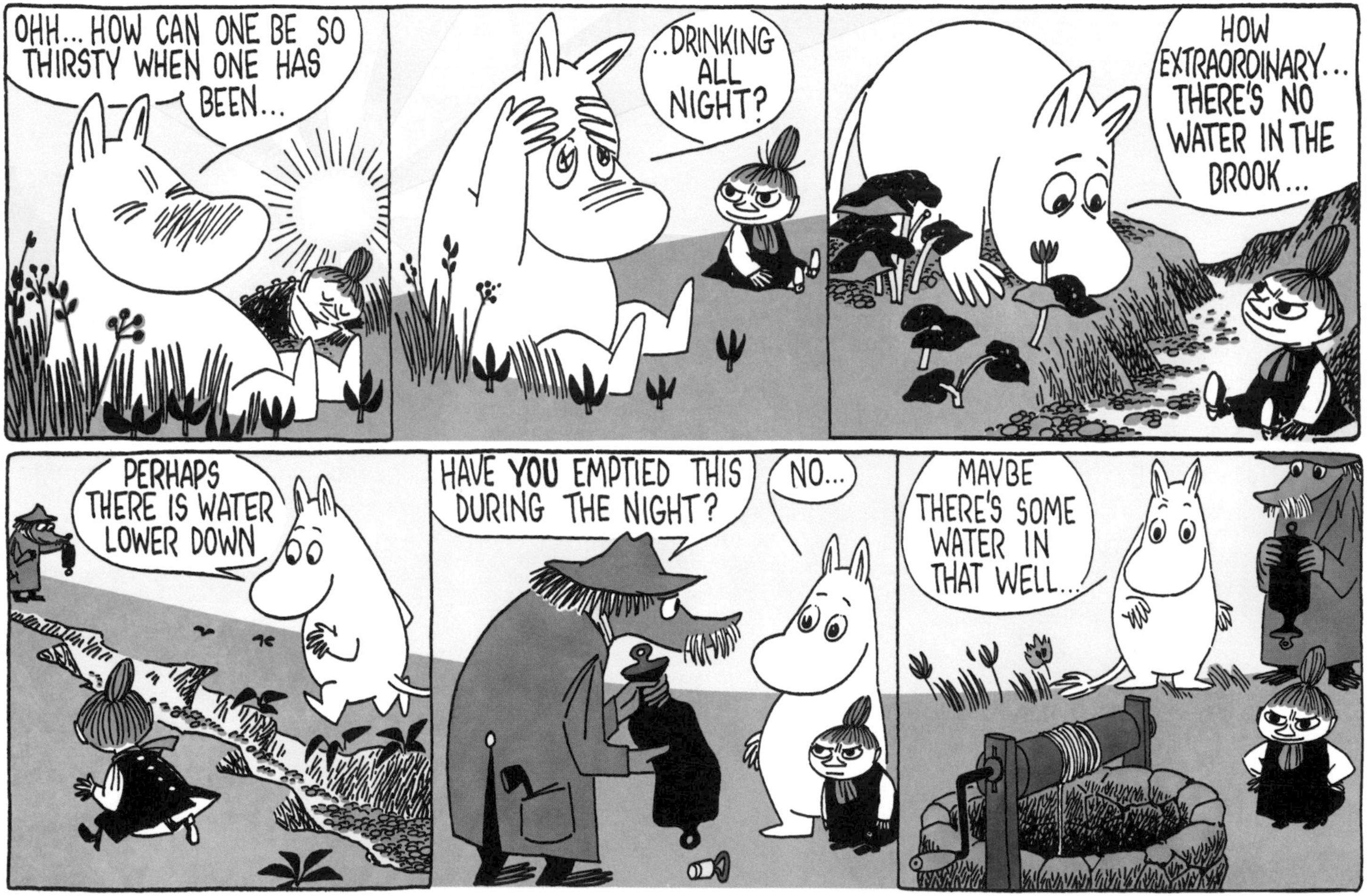
OHH... HOW CAN ONE BE SO THIRSTY WHEN ONE HAS BEEN...
..DRINKING ALL NIGHT?
HOW EXTRAORDINARY... THERE'S NO WATER IN THE BROOK...
PERHAPS THERE IS WATER LOWER DOWN
HAVE **YOU** EMPTIED THIS DURING THE NIGHT?
NO...
MAYBE THERE'S SOME WATER IN THAT WELL...

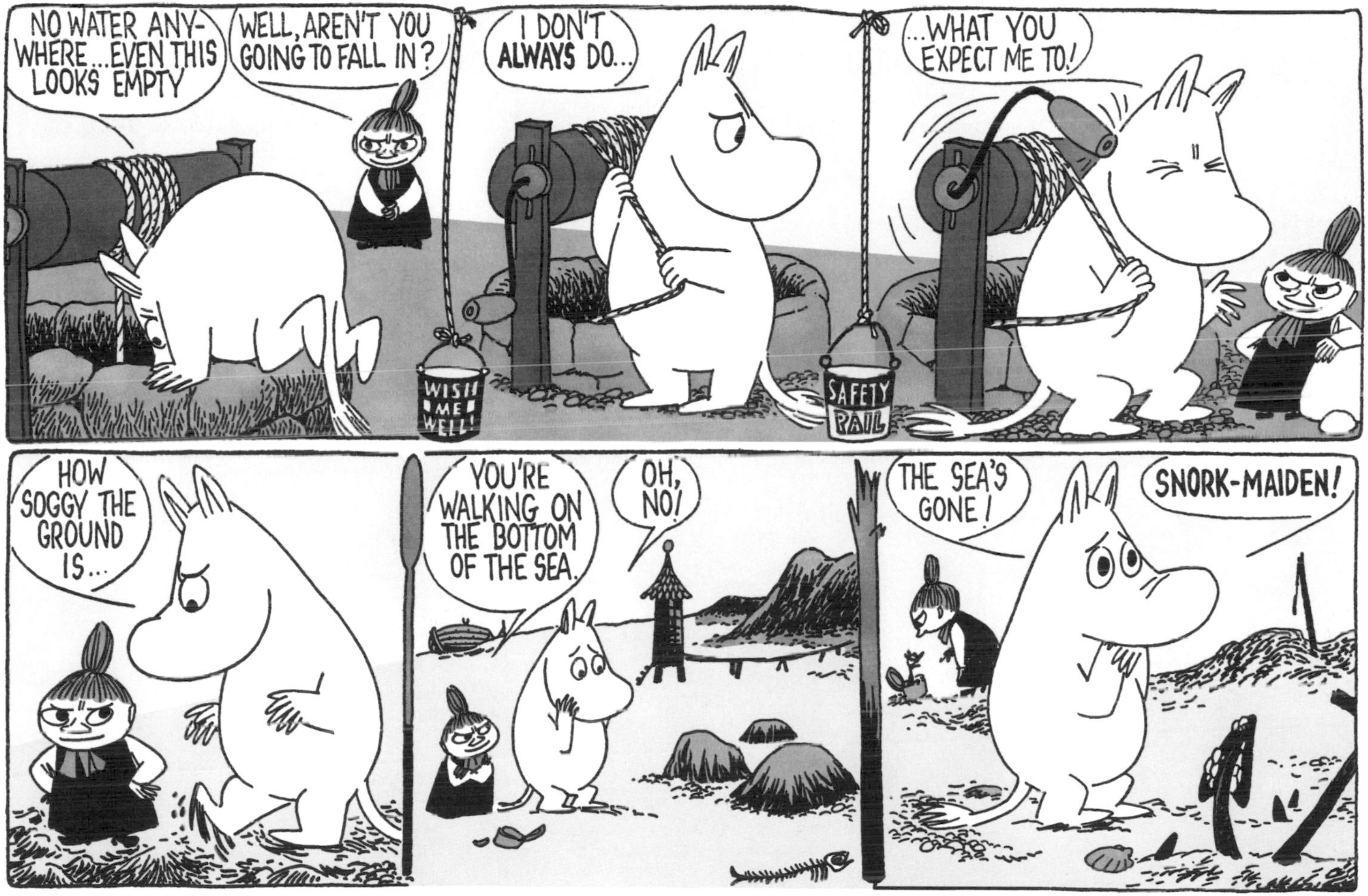
NO WATER ANY-WHERE...EVEN THIS LOOKS EMPTY
WELL, AREN'T YOU GOING TO FALL IN?
WISH ME WELL!
I DON'T **ALWAYS** DO...
...WHAT YOU EXPECT ME TO!
SAFETY PAIL
HOW SOGGY THE GROUND IS...
YOU'RE WALKING ON THE BOTTOM OF THE SEA.
OH, NO!
THE SEA'S GONE!
SNORK-MAIDEN!

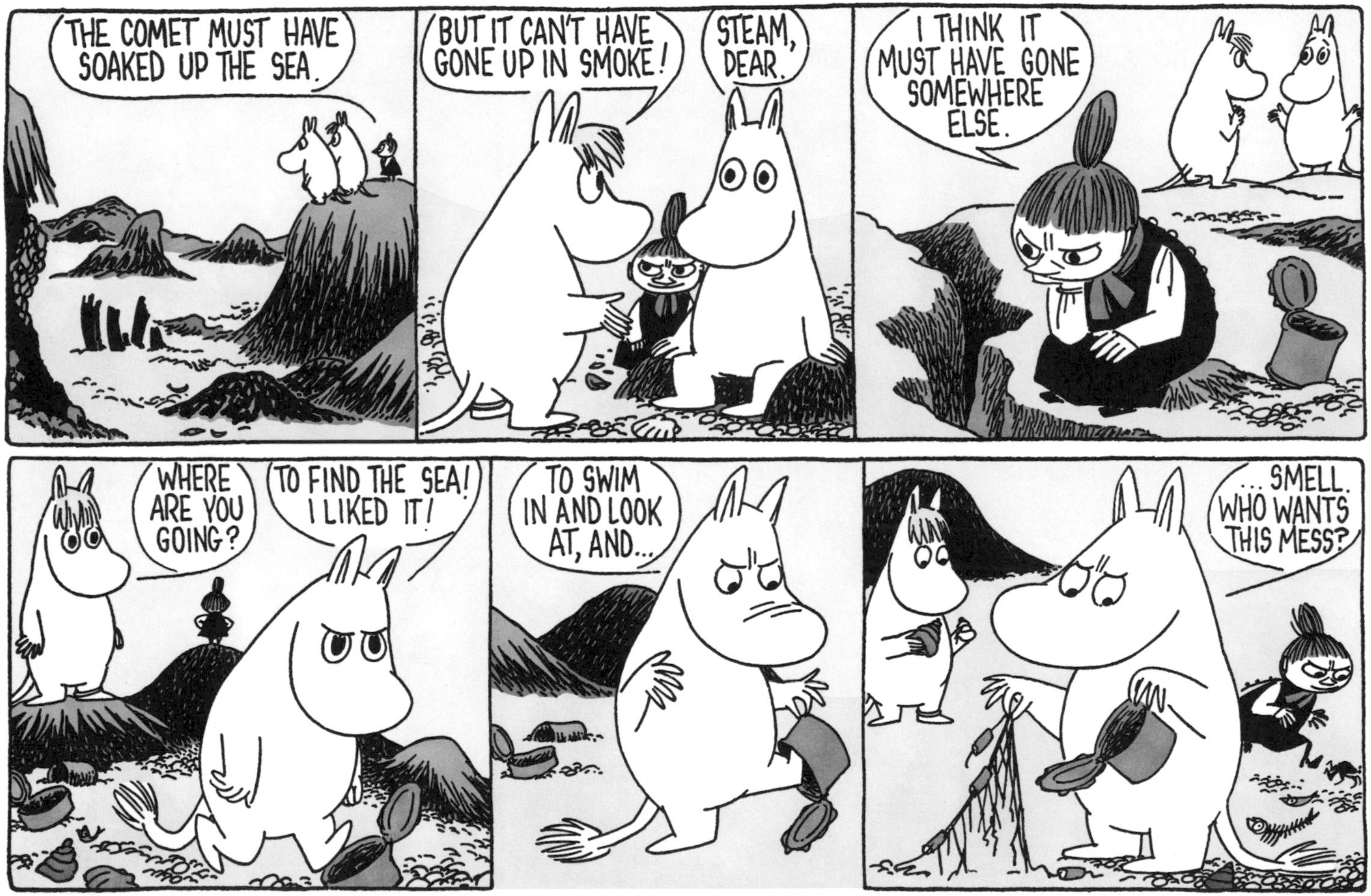
THE COMET MUST HAVE SOAKED UP THE SEA.
BUT IT CAN'T HAVE GONE UP IN SMOKE!
STEAM, DEAR.
I THINK IT MUST HAVE GONE SOMEWHERE ELSE.
WHERE ARE YOU GOING?
TO FIND THE SEA! I LIKED IT!
TO SWIM IN AND LOOK AT, AND...
... SMELL. WHO WANTS THIS MESS?

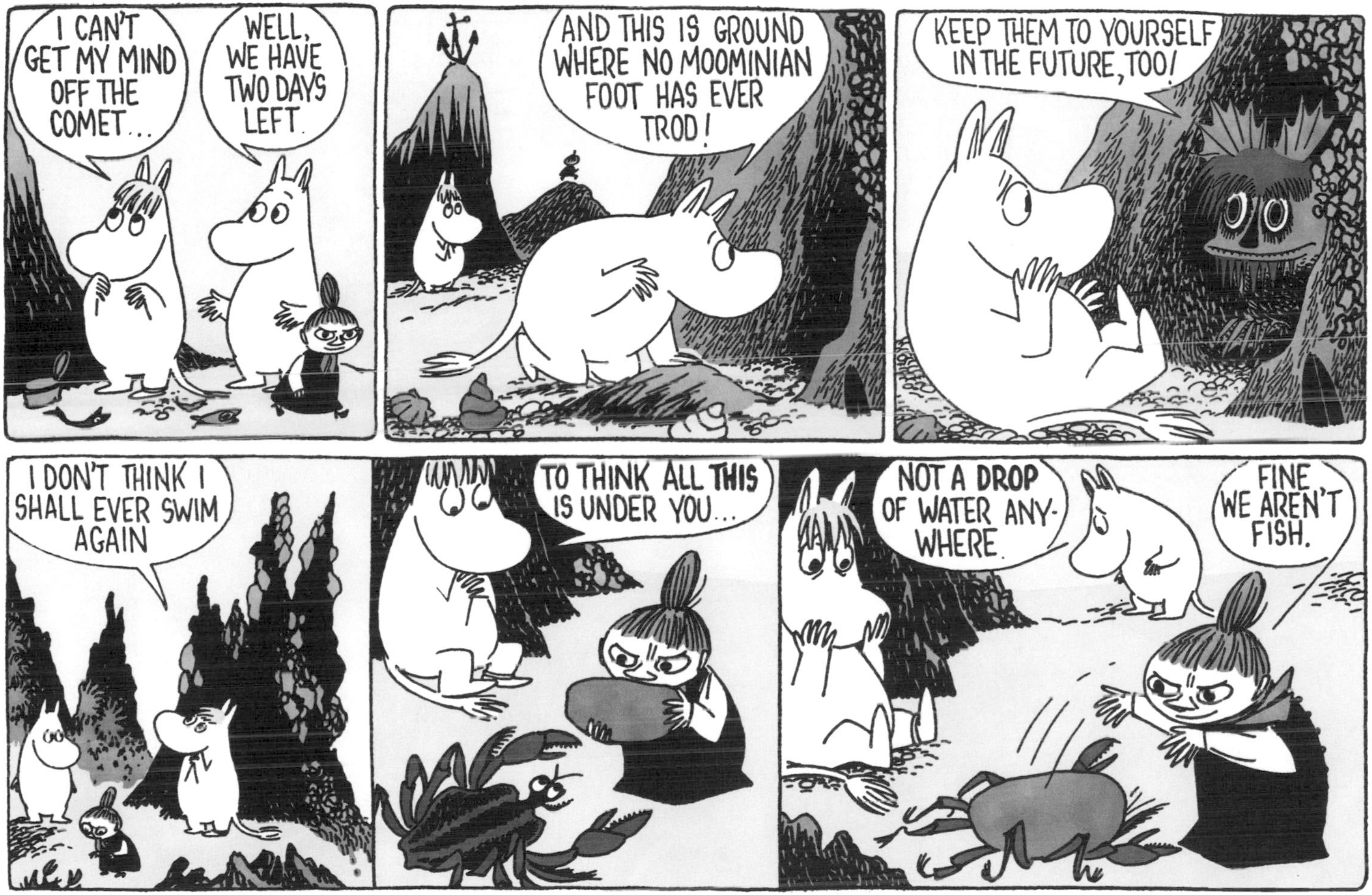
I CAN'T GET MY MIND OFF THE COMET...
WELL, WE HAVE TWO DAYS LEFT.
AND THIS IS GROUND WHERE NO MOOMINIAN FOOT HAS EVER TROD!
KEEP THEM TO YOURSELF IN THE FUTURE, TOO!
I DON'T THINK I SHALL EVER SWIM AGAIN
TO THINK ALL **THIS** IS UNDER YOU...
NOT A **DROP** OF WATER ANYWHERE.
FINE WE AREN'T FISH.

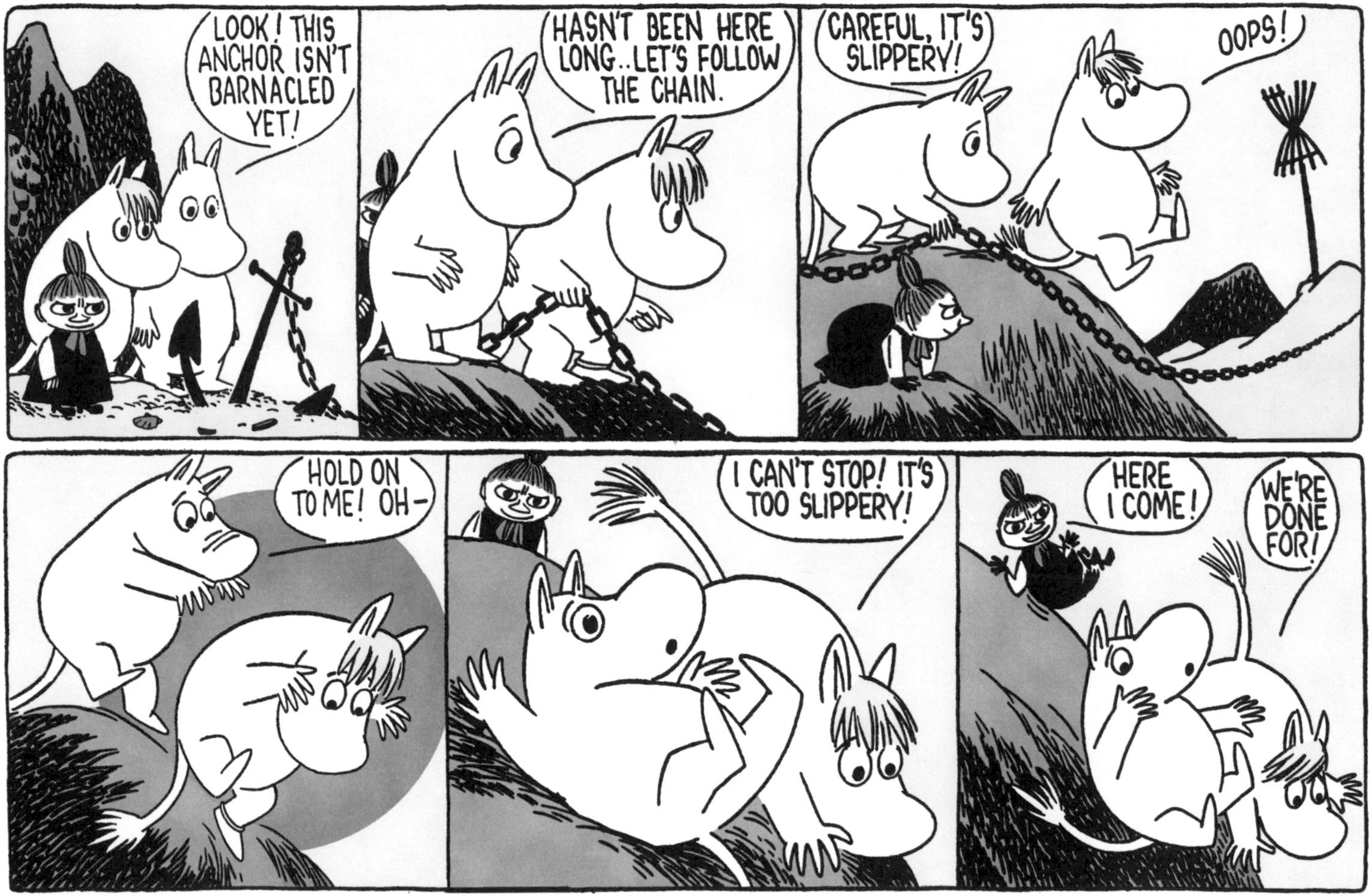
LOOK! THIS ANCHOR ISN'T BARNACLED YET!
HASN'T BEEN HERE LONG..LET'S FOLLOW THE CHAIN.
CAREFUL, IT'S SLIPPERY!
OOPS!
HOLD ON TO ME! OH-
I CAN'T STOP! IT'S TOO SLIPPERY!
HERE I COME!
WE'RE DONE FOR!

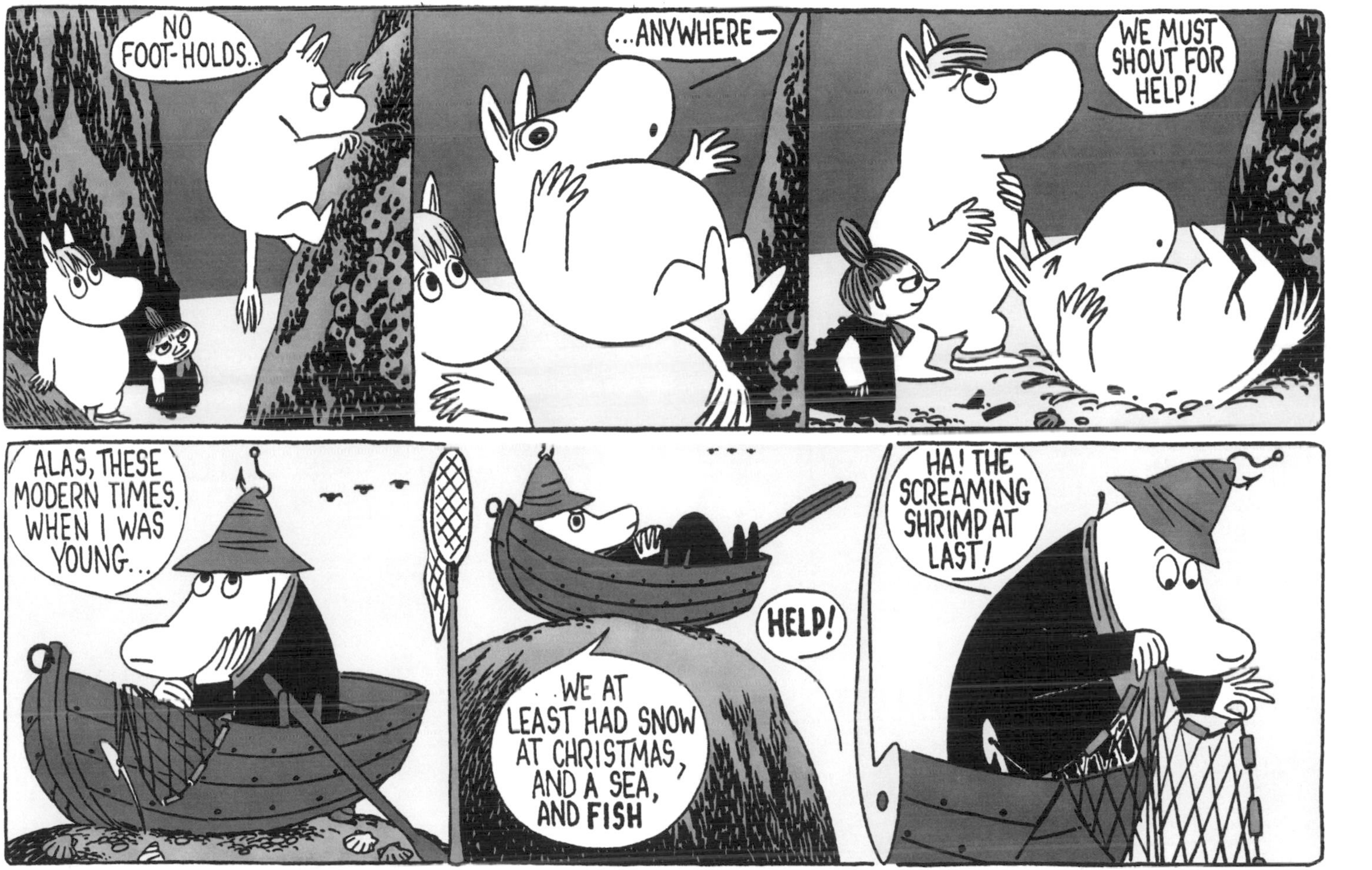

NO FOOT-HOLDS..
...ANYWHERE—
WE MUST SHOUT FOR HELP!
ALAS, THESE MODERN TIMES. WHEN I WAS YOUNG...
..WE AT LEAST HAD SNOW AT CHRISTMAS, AND A SEA, AND **FISH**
HELP!
HA! THE SCREAMING SHRIMP AT LAST!

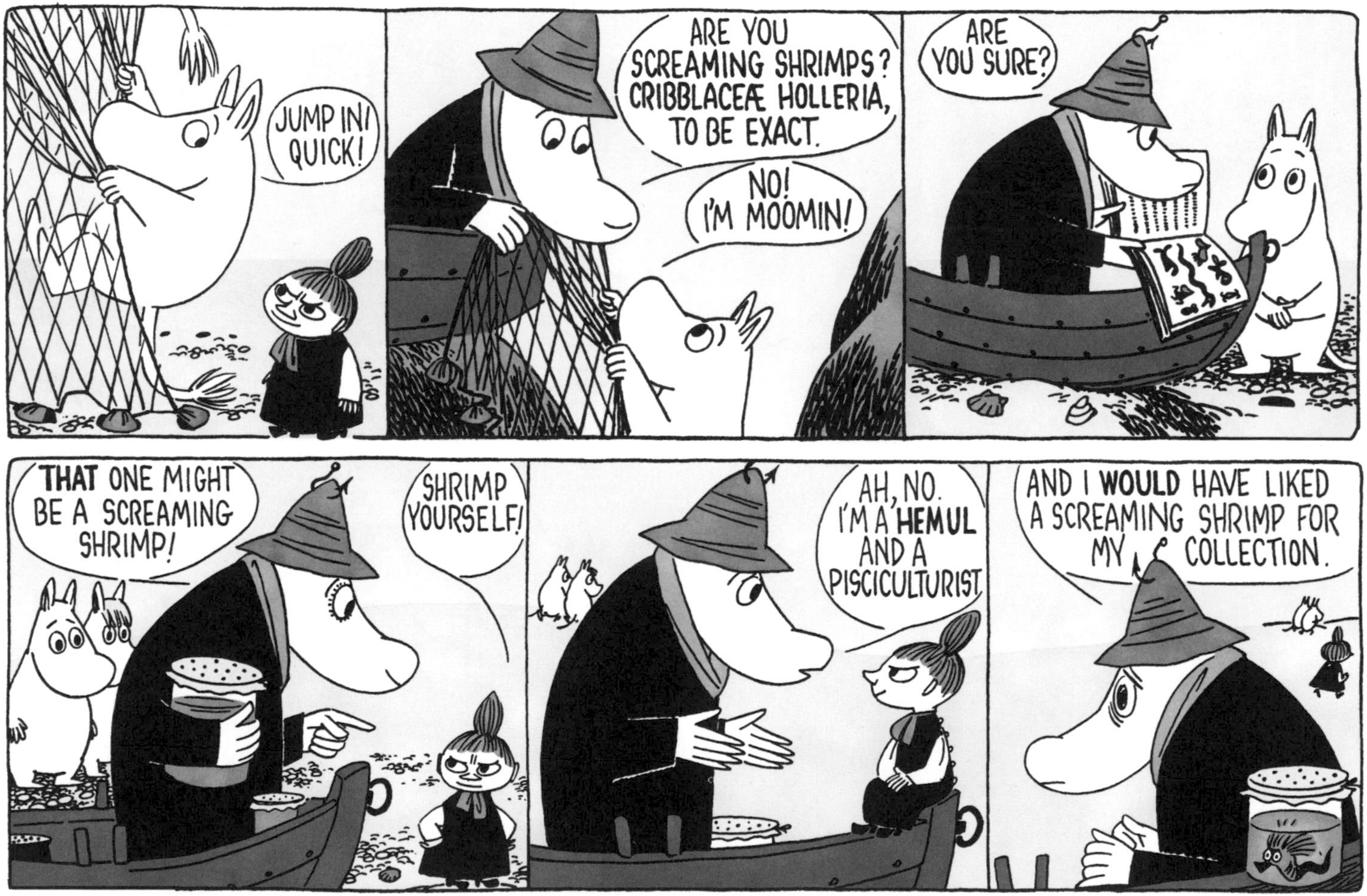
JUMP IN! QUICK!
ARE YOU SCREAMING SHRIMPS? CRIBBLACEÆ HOLLERIA, TO BE EXACT.
NO! I'M MOOMIN!
ARE YOU SURE?
THAT ONE MIGHT BE A SCREAMING SHRIMP!
SHRIMP YOURSELF!
AH, NO. I'M A **HEMUL** AND A PISCICULTURIST.
AND I **WOULD** HAVE LIKED A SCREAMING SHRIMP FOR MY COLLECTION.

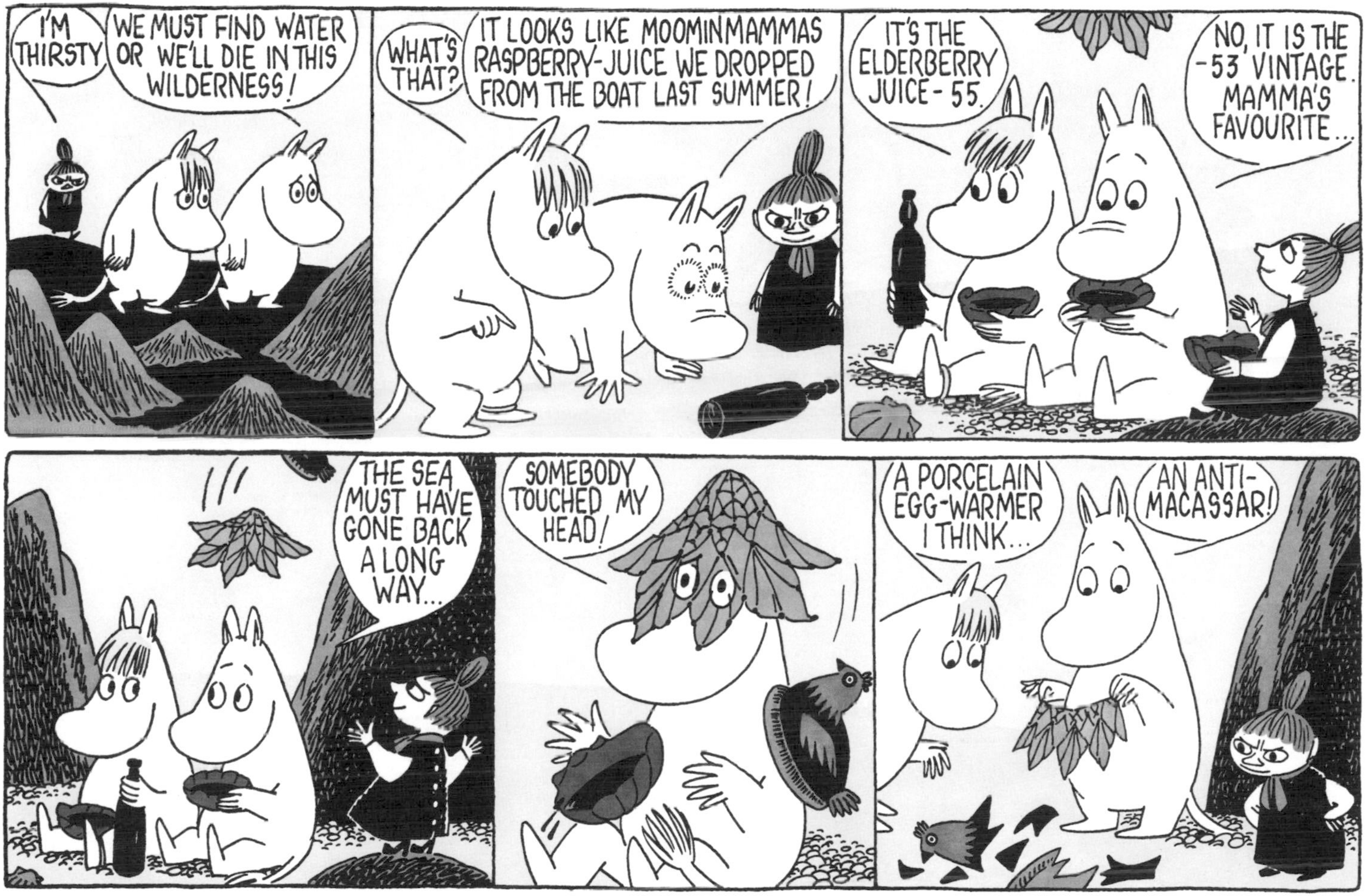
I'M THIRSTY
WE MUST FIND WATER OR WE'LL DIE IN THIS WILDERNESS!
WHAT'S THAT?
IT LOOKS LIKE MOOMINMAMMAS RASPBERRY-JUICE WE DROPPED FROM THE BOAT LAST SUMMER!
IT'S THE ELDERBERRY JUICE-55.
NO, IT IS THE -53 VINTAGE. MAMMA'S FAVOURITE...
THE SEA MUST HAVE GONE BACK A LONG WAY...
SOMEBODY TOUCHED MY HEAD!
A PORCELAIN EGG-WARMER I THINK...
AN ANTI-MACASSAR!

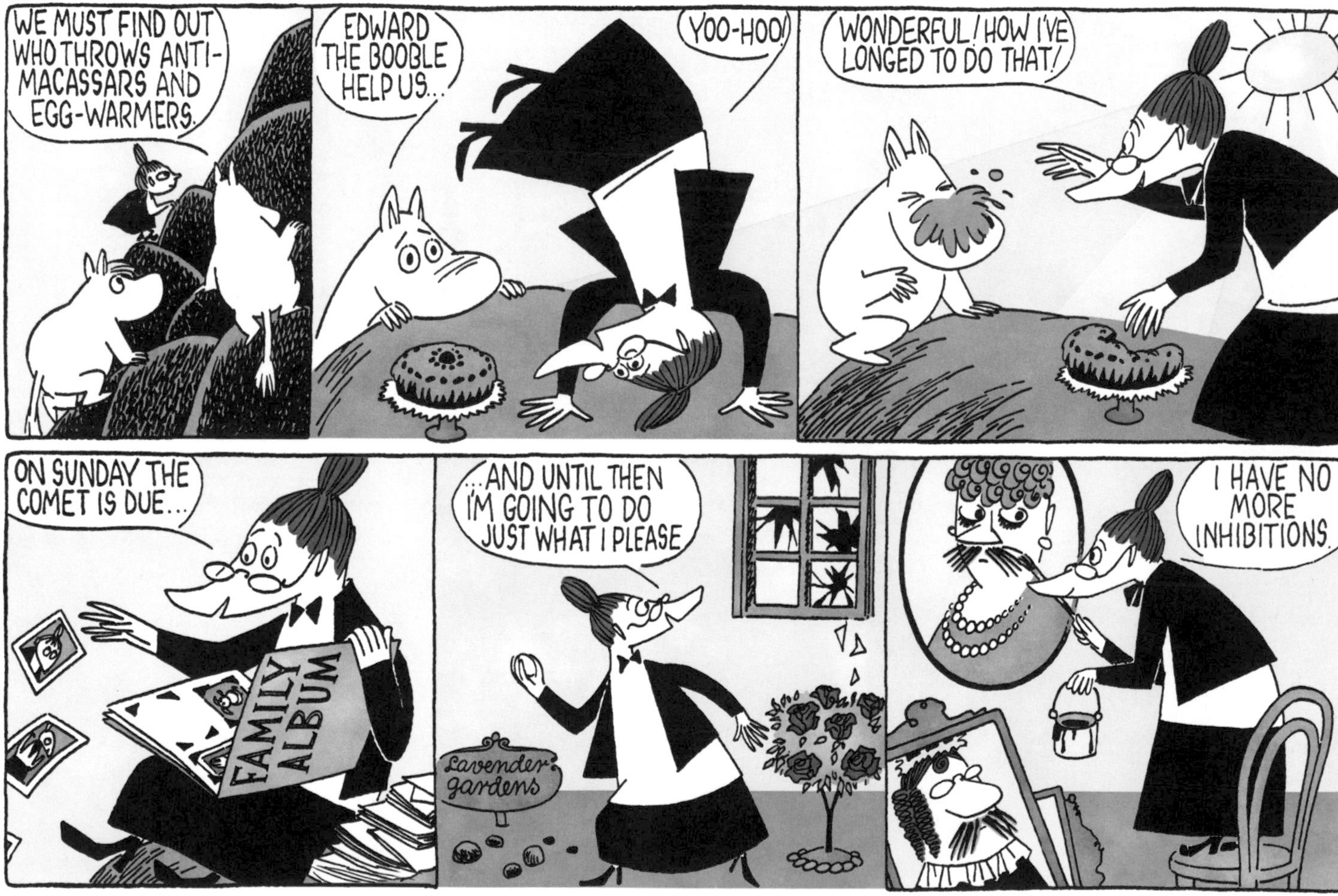
WE MUST FIND OUT WHO THROWS ANTI-MACASSARS AND EGG-WARMERS.
EDWARD THE BOOBLE HELP US...
YOO-HOO!
WONDERFUL! HOW I'VE LONGED TO DO THAT!
ON SUNDAY THE COMET IS DUE...
FAMILY ALBUM
...AND UNTIL THEN I'M GOING TO DO JUST WHAT I PLEASE
Lavender gardens
I HAVE NO MORE INHIBITIONS.

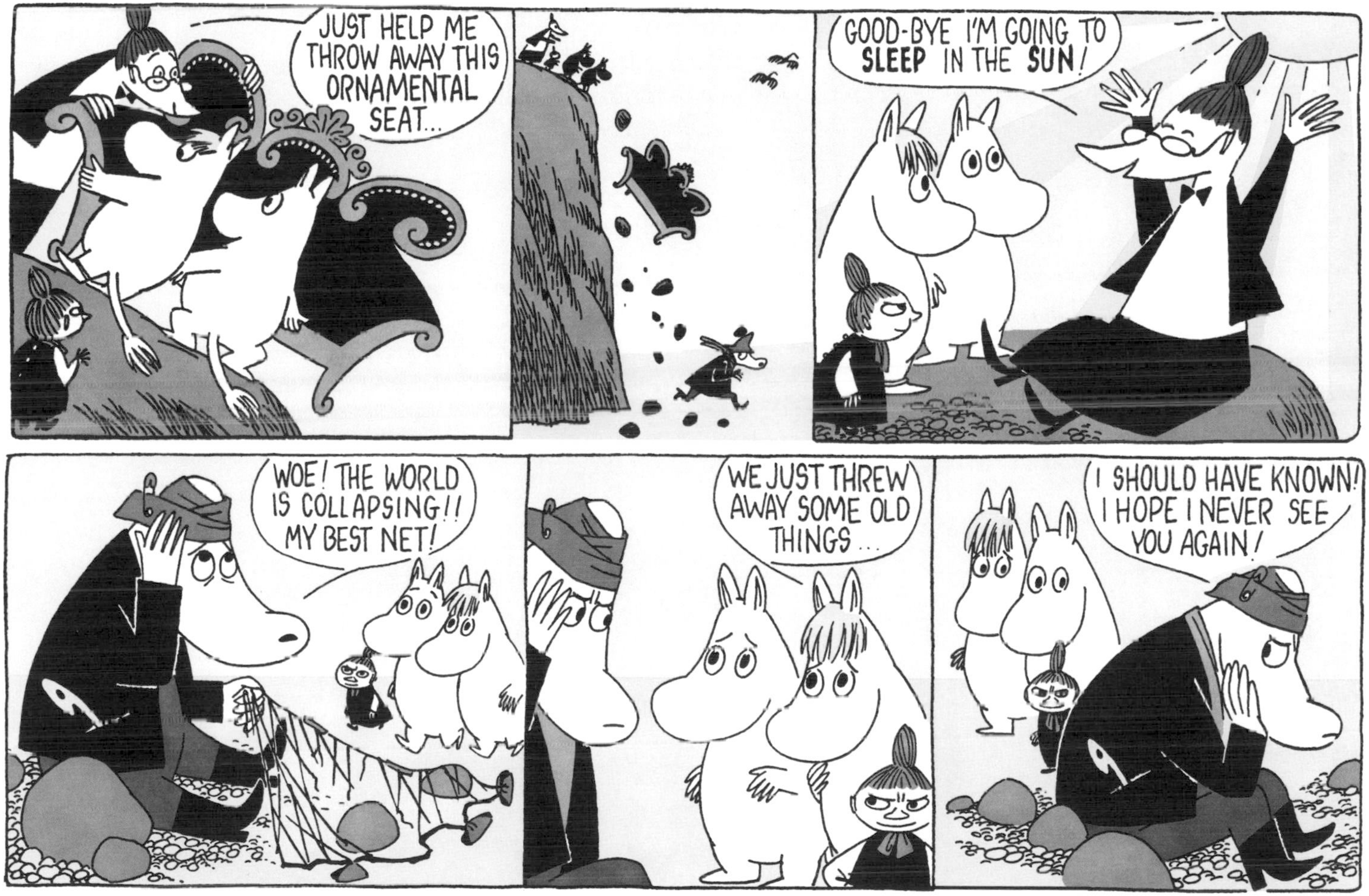
JUST HELP ME THROW AWAY THIS ORNAMENTAL SEAT...
GOOD-BYE I'M GOING TO **SLEEP** IN THE **SUN**!
WOE! THE WORLD IS COLLAPSING!! MY BEST NET!
WE JUST THREW AWAY SOME OLD THINGS ...
I SHOULD HAVE KNOWN! I HOPE I NEVER SEE YOU AGAIN!

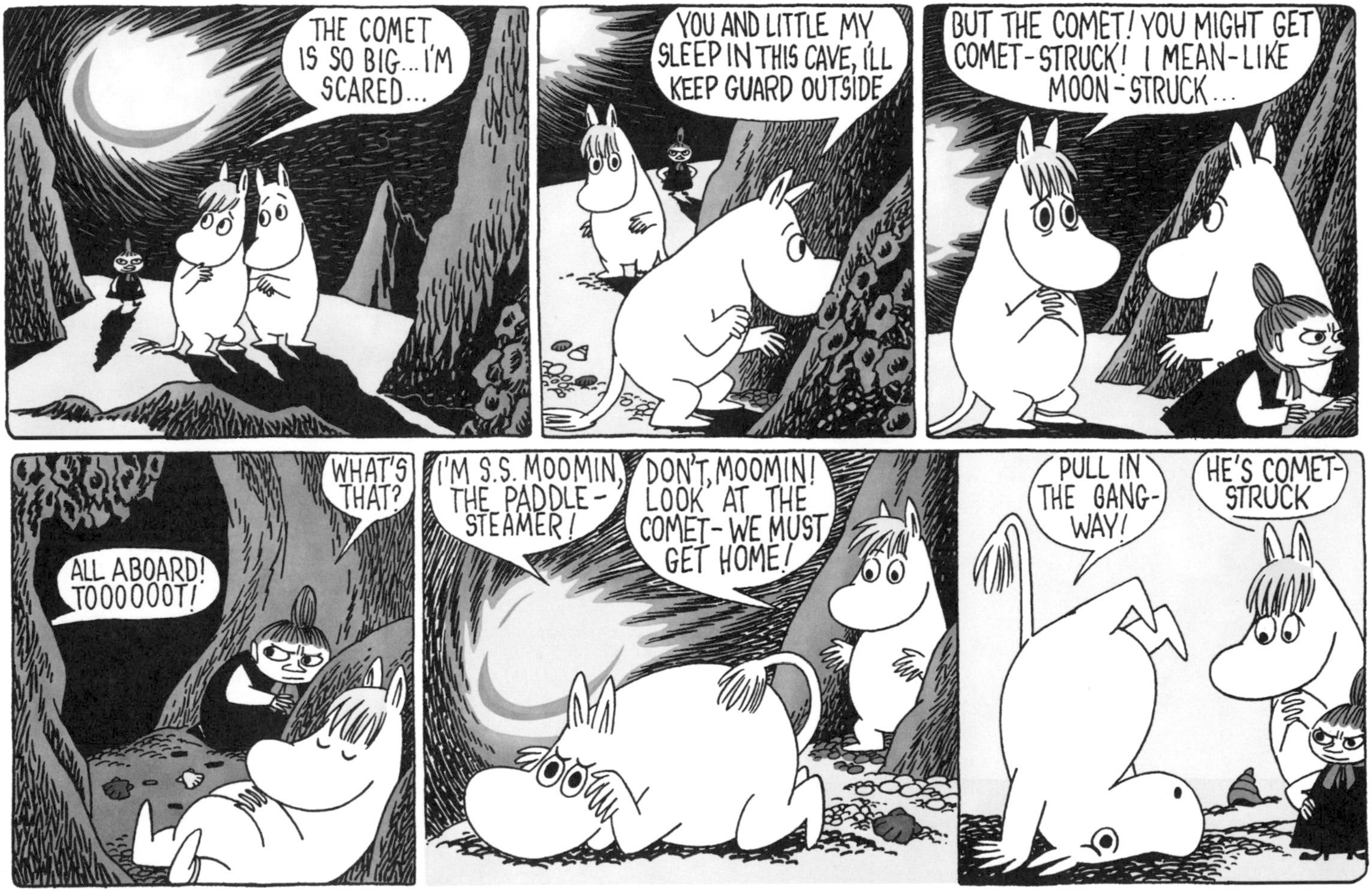
THE COMET IS SO BIG... I'M SCARED...
YOU AND LITTLE MY SLEEP IN THIS CAVE, I'LL KEEP GUARD OUTSIDE
BUT THE COMET! YOU MIGHT GET COMET-STRUCK! I MEAN-LIKE MOON-STRUCK...
WHAT'S THAT?
ALL ABOARD! TOOOOOOT!
I'M S.S. MOOMIN, THE PADDLE-STEAMER!
DON'T, MOOMIN! LOOK AT THE COMET-WE MUST GET HOME!
PULL IN THE GANG-WAY!
HE'S COMET-STRUCK

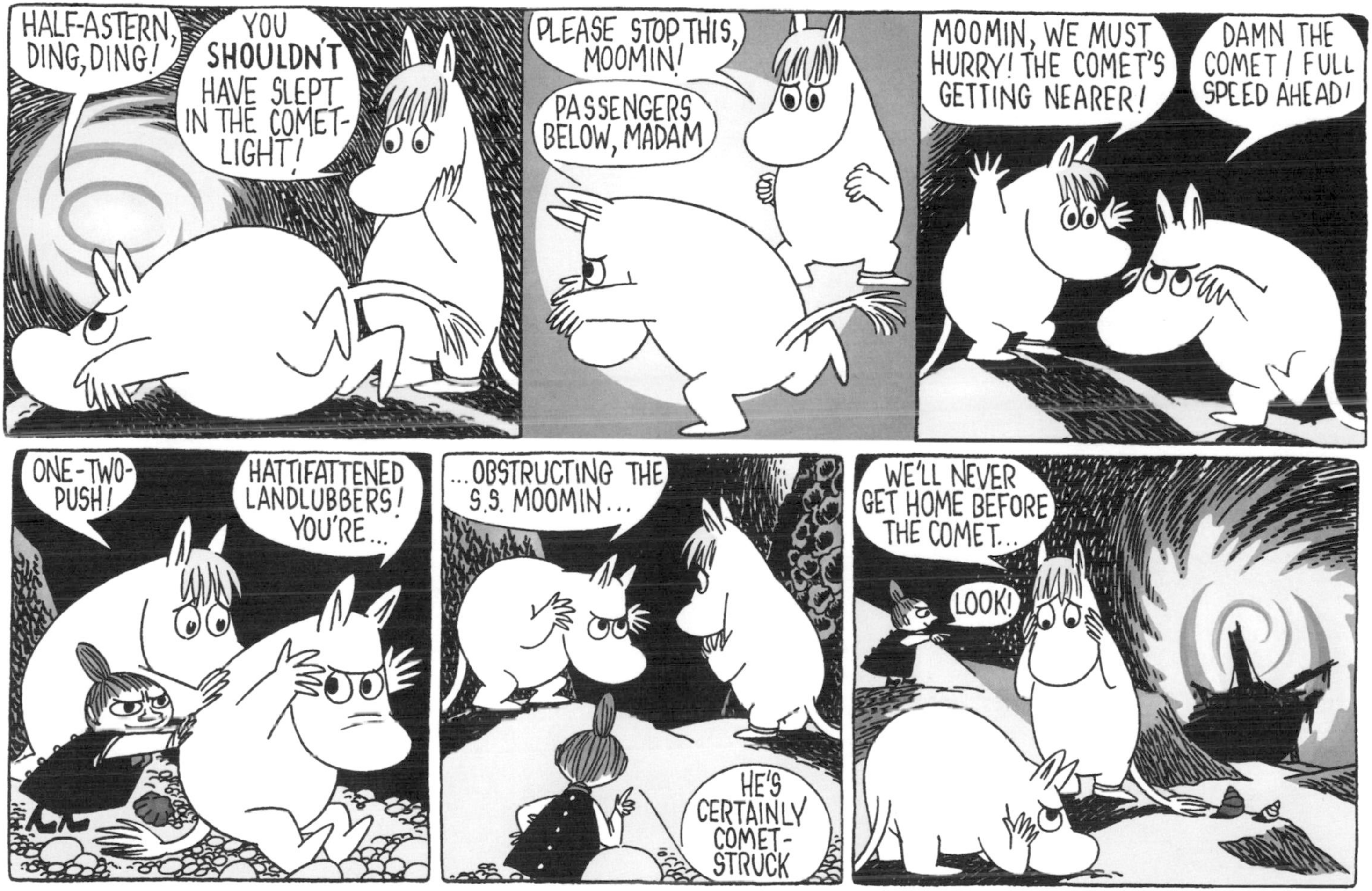

HALF-ASTERN, DING, DING!
YOU **SHOULDN'T** HAVE SLEPT IN THE COMET-LIGHT!
PLEASE STOP THIS, MOOMIN!
PASSENGERS BELOW, MADAM
MOOMIN, WE MUST HURRY! THE COMET'S GETTING NEARER!
DAMN THE COMET! FULL SPEED AHEAD!
ONE-TWO-PUSH!
HATTIFATTENED LANDLUBBERS! YOU'RE...
...OBSTRUCTING THE S.S. MOOMIN...
HE'S CERTAINLY COMET-STRUCK
WE'LL NEVER GET HOME BEFORE THE COMET...
LOOK!

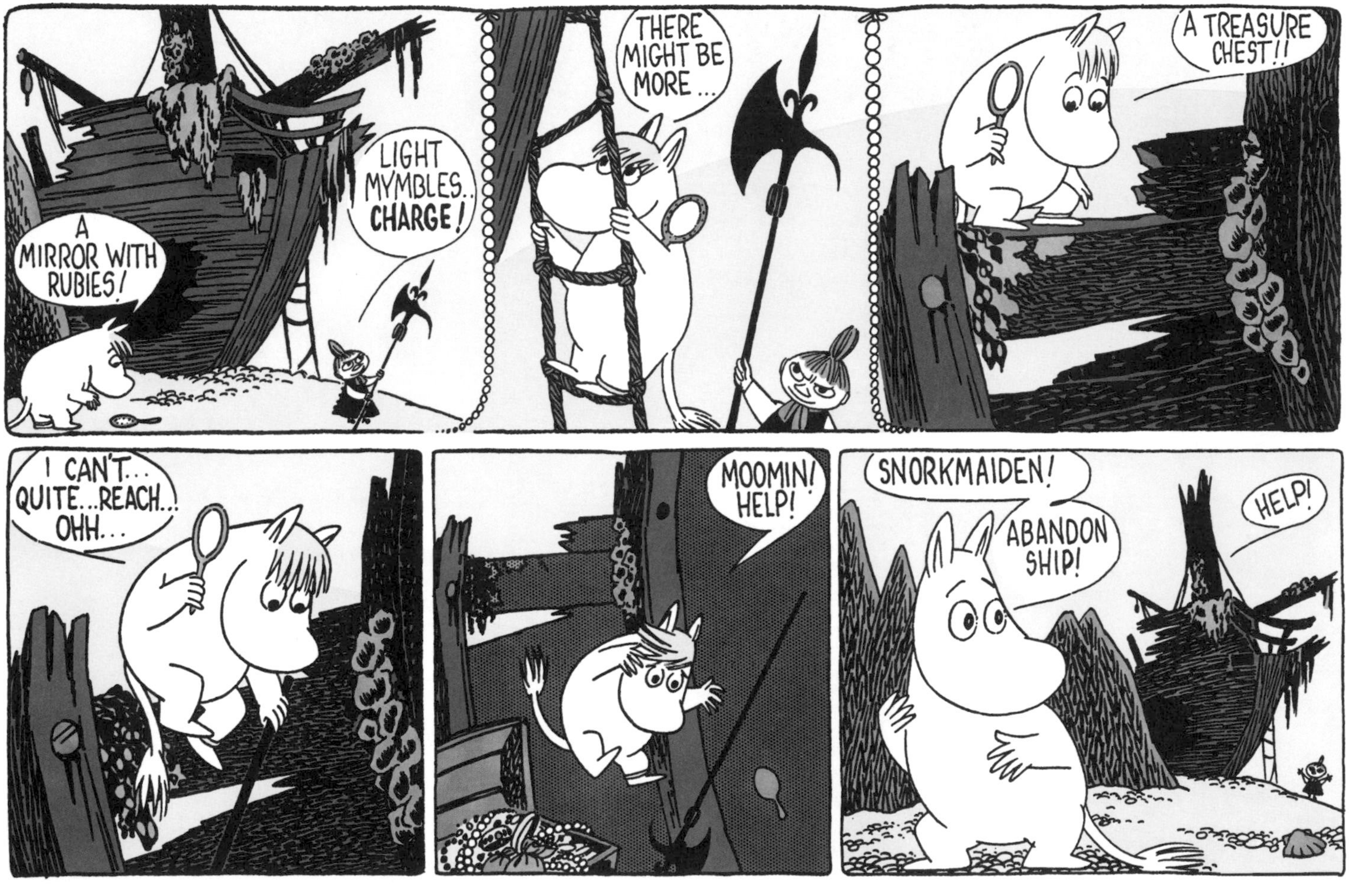
A MIRROR WITH RUBIES!
LIGHT MYMBLES... CHARGE!
THERE MIGHT BE MORE...
A TREASURE CHEST!!
I CAN'T... QUITE...REACH... OHH...
MOOMIN! HELP!
SNORKMAIDEN!
ABANDON SHIP!
HELP!

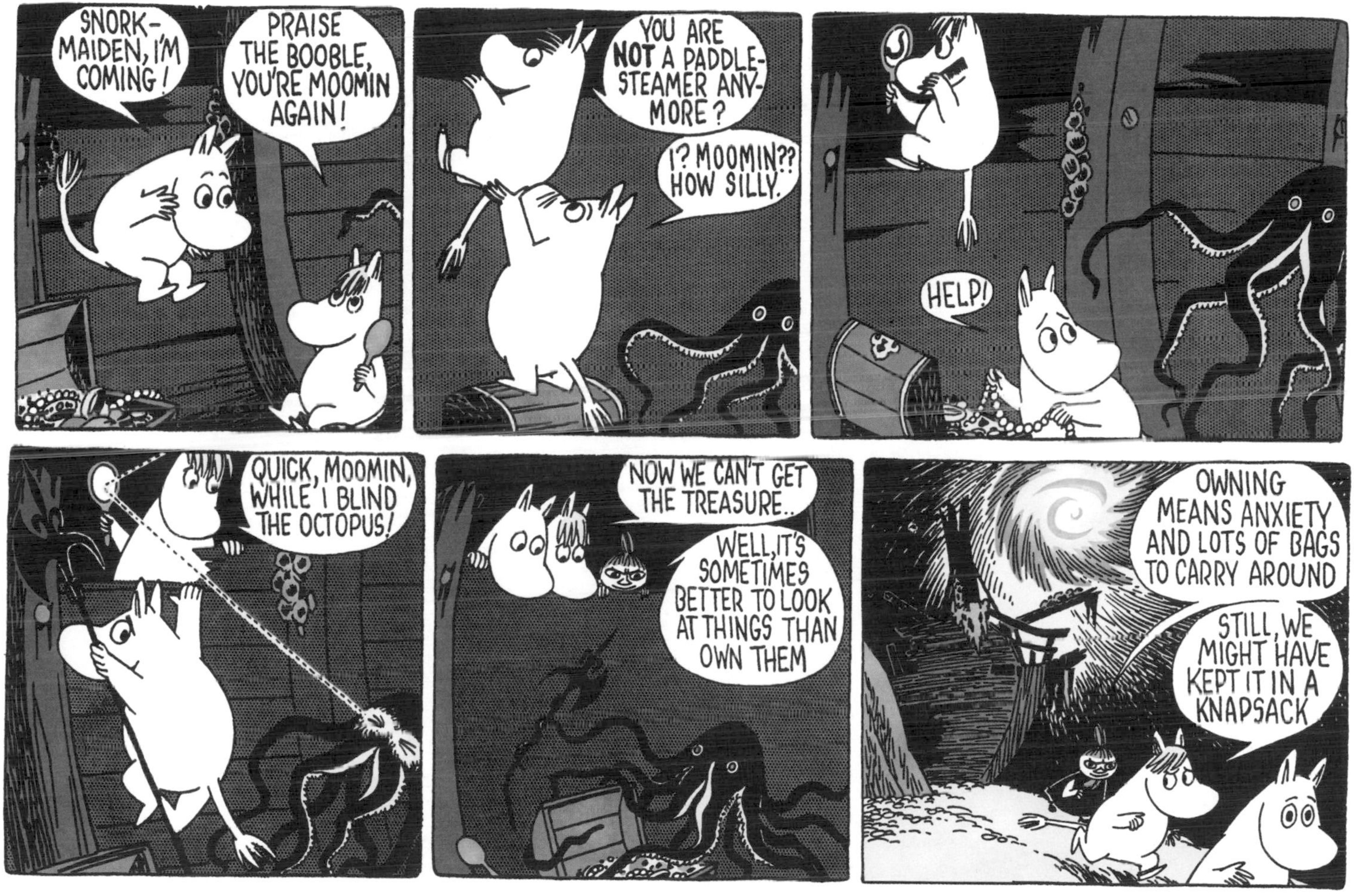
SNORK-MAIDEN, I'M COMING!
PRAISE THE BOOBLE, YOU'RE MOOMIN AGAIN!
YOU ARE NOT A PADDLE-STEAMER ANY-MORE?
I? MOOMIN?? HOW SILLY.
HELP!
QUICK, MOOMIN, WHILE I BLIND THE OCTOPUS!
NOW WE CAN'T GET THE TREASURE..
WELL, IT'S SOMETIMES BETTER TO LOOK AT THINGS THAN OWN THEM
OWNING MEANS ANXIETY AND LOTS OF BAGS TO CARRY AROUND
STILL, WE MIGHT HAVE KEPT IT IN A KNAPSACK

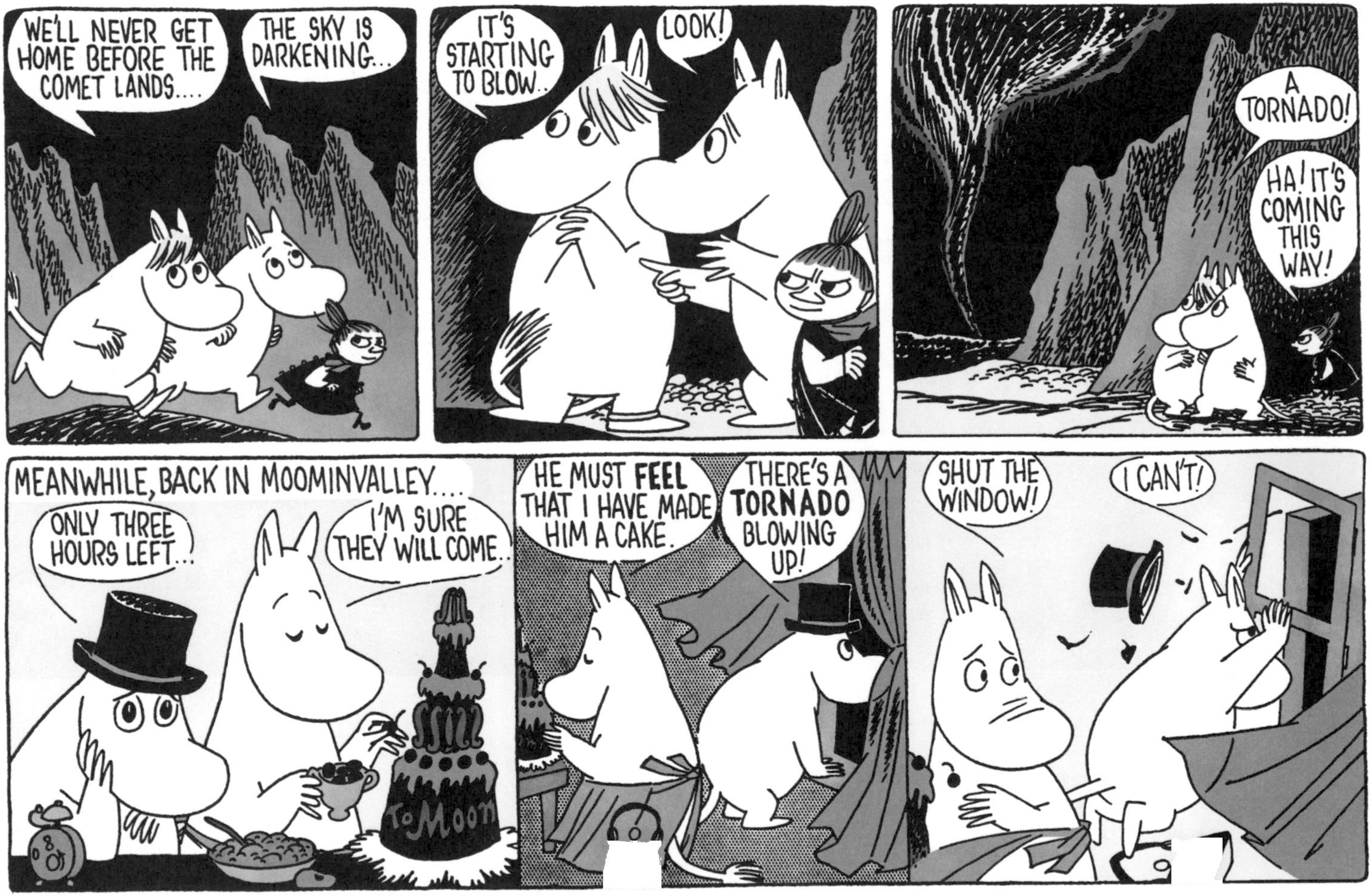
WE'LL NEVER GET HOME BEFORE THE COMET LANDS....
THE SKY IS DARKENING...
IT'S STARTING TO BLOW..
LOOK!
A TORNADO!
HA! IT'S COMING THIS WAY!
MEANWHILE, BACK IN MOOMINVALLEY....
ONLY THREE HOURS LEFT...
I'M SURE THEY WILL COME...
TO MOOM
HE MUST FEEL THAT I HAVE MADE HIM A CAKE.
THERE'S A TORNADO BLOWING UP!
SHUT THE WINDOW!
I CAN'T!

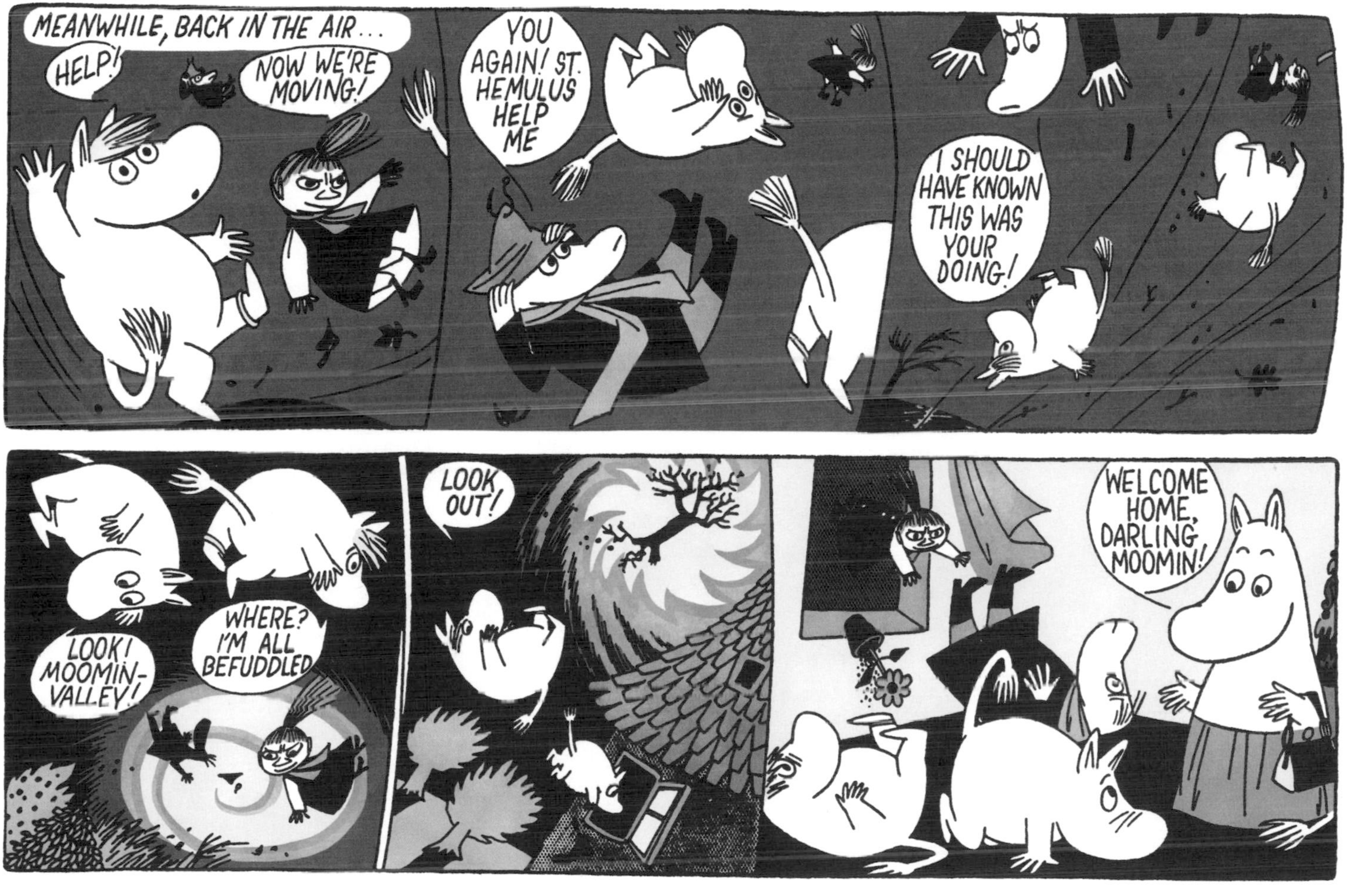
MEANWHILE, BACK IN THE AIR...
HELP!
NOW WE'RE MOVING!
YOU AGAIN! ST. HEMULUS HELP ME
I SHOULD HAVE KNOWN THIS WAS YOUR DOING!
LOOK! MOOMIN-VALLEY!
WHERE? I'M ALL BEFUDDLED
LOOK OUT!
WELCOME HOME, DARLING MOOMIN!

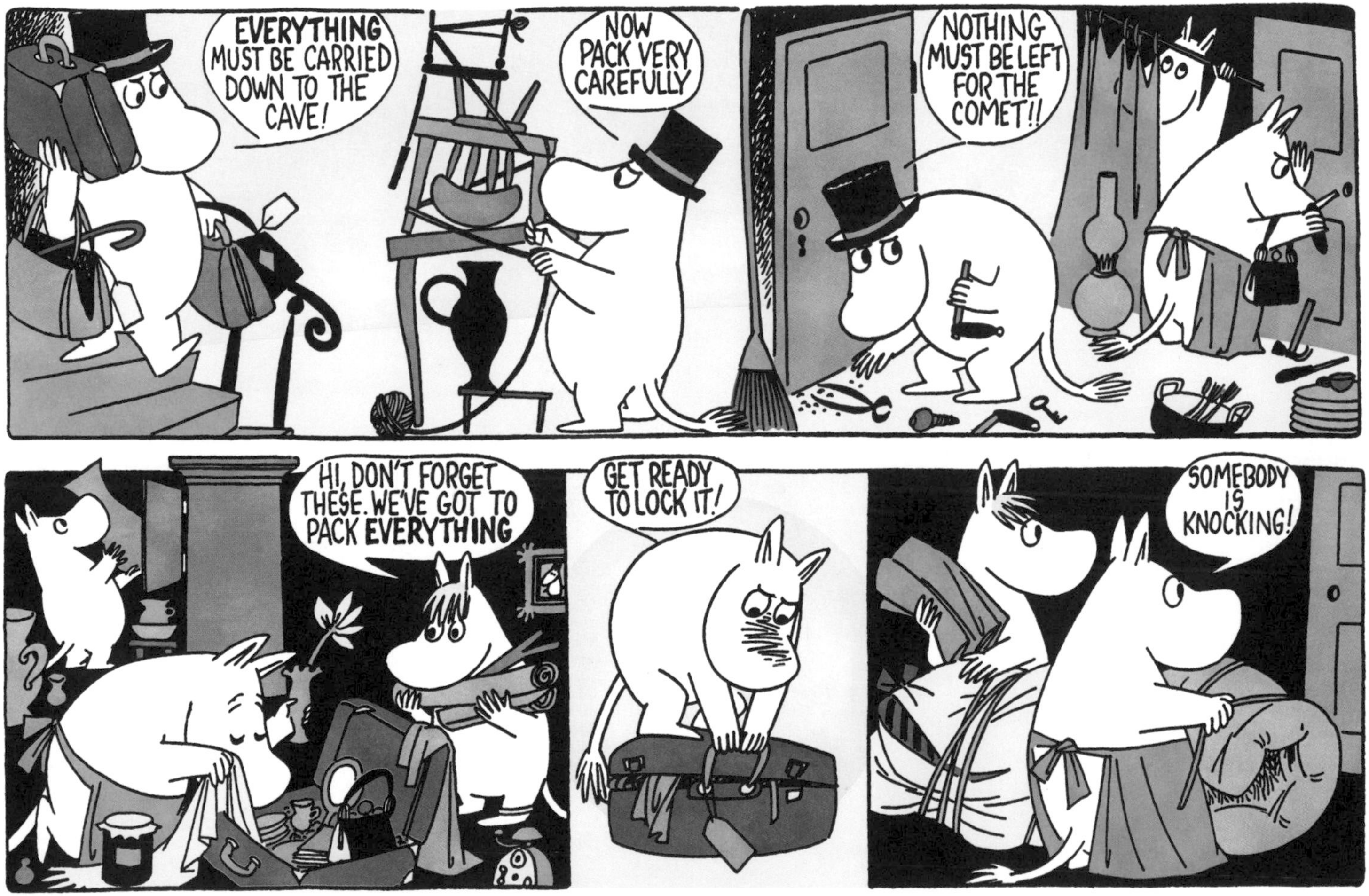
EVERYTHING MUST BE CARRIED DOWN TO THE CAVE!
NOW PACK VERY CAREFULLY
NOTHING MUST BE LEFT FOR THE COMET!!
HI, DON'T FORGET THESE. WE'VE GOT TO PACK EVERYTHING
GET READY TO LOCK IT!
SOMEBODY IS KNOCKING!

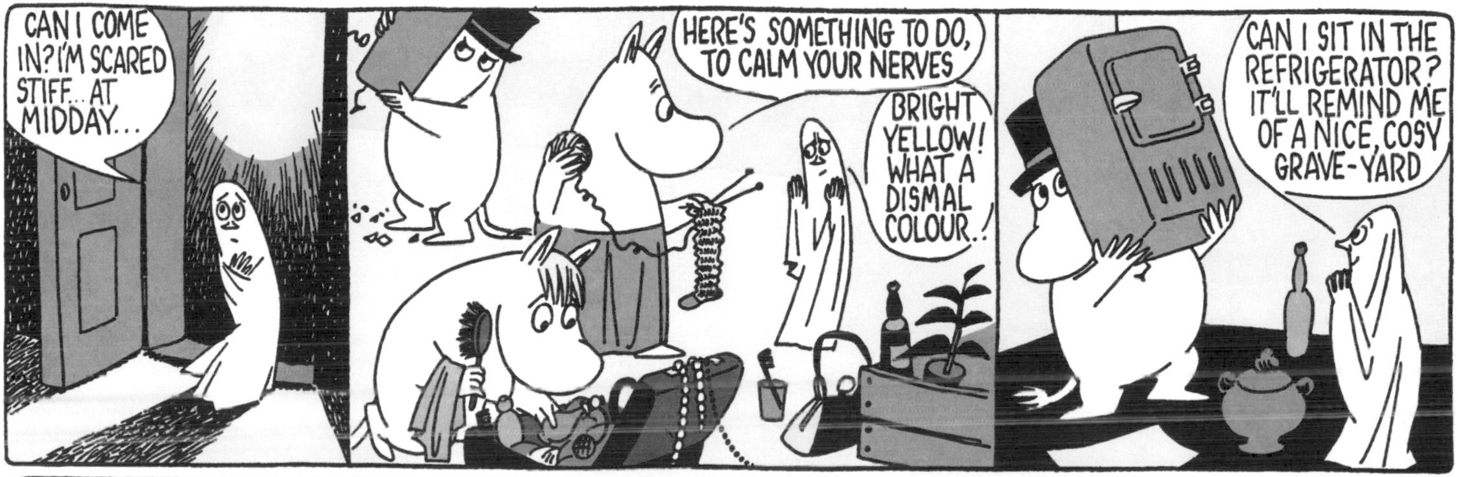
CAN I COME IN? I'M SCARED STIFF... AT MIDDAY...
HERE'S SOMETHING TO DO, TO CALM YOUR NERVES
BRIGHT YELLOW! WHAT A DISMAL COLOUR..!
CAN I SIT IN THE REFRIGERATOR? IT'LL REMIND ME OF A NICE, COSY GRAVE-YARD

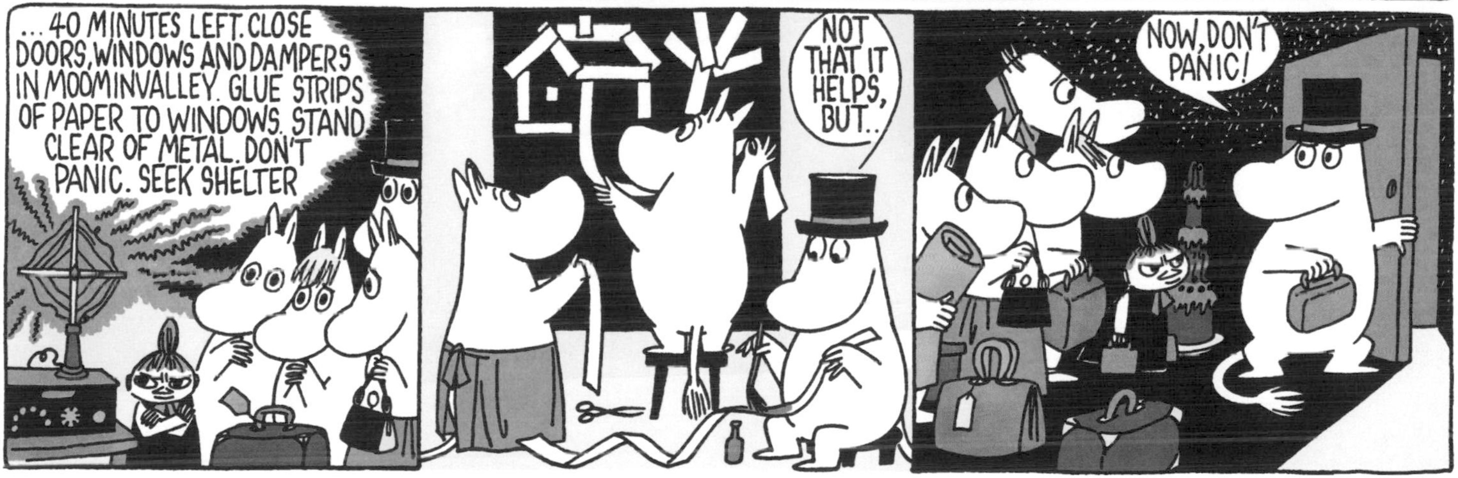
...40 MINUTES LEFT. CLOSE DOORS, WINDOWS AND DAMPERS IN MOOMINVALLEY. GLUE STRIPS OF PAPER TO WINDOWS. STAND CLEAR OF METAL. DON'T PANIC. SEEK SHELTER
NOT THAT IT HELPS, BUT..
NOW, DON'T PANIC!

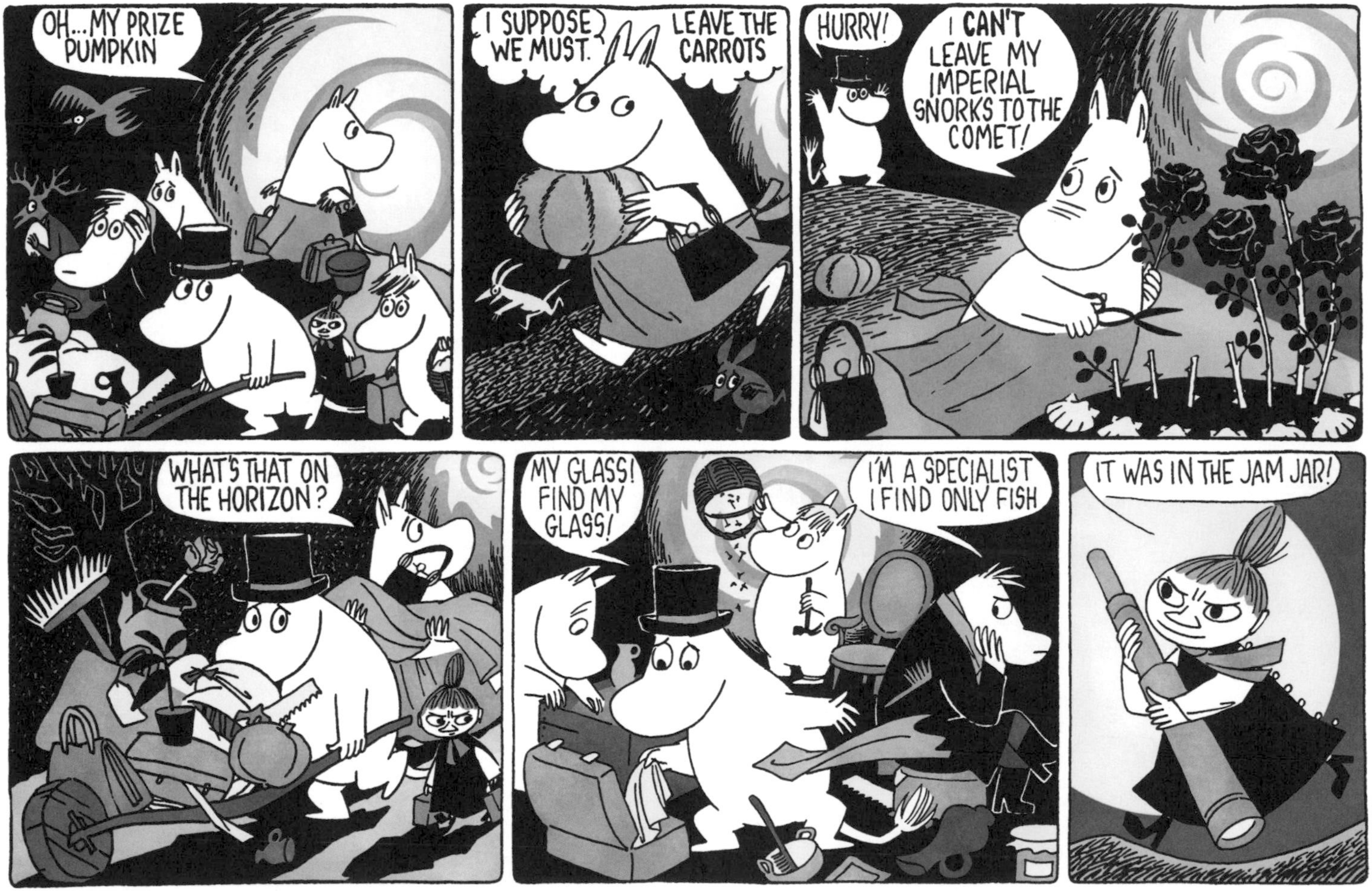
OH... MY PRIZE PUMPKIN
I SUPPOSE WE MUST.
LEAVE THE CARROTS
HURRY!
I CAN'T LEAVE MY IMPERIAL SNORKS TO THE COMET!
WHAT'S THAT ON THE HORIZON?
MY GLASS! FIND MY GLASS!
I'M A SPECIALIST I FIND ONLY FISH
IT WAS IN THE JAM JAR!

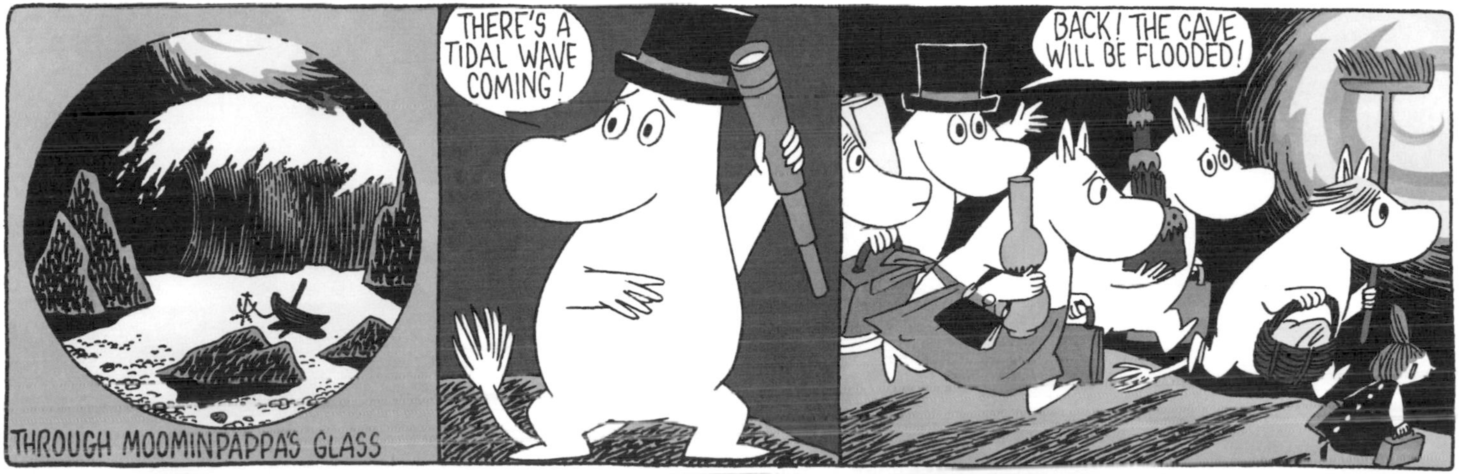
THROUGH MOOMINPAPPA'S GLASS
THERE'S A TIDAL WAVE COMING!
BACK! THE CAVE WILL BE FLOODED!

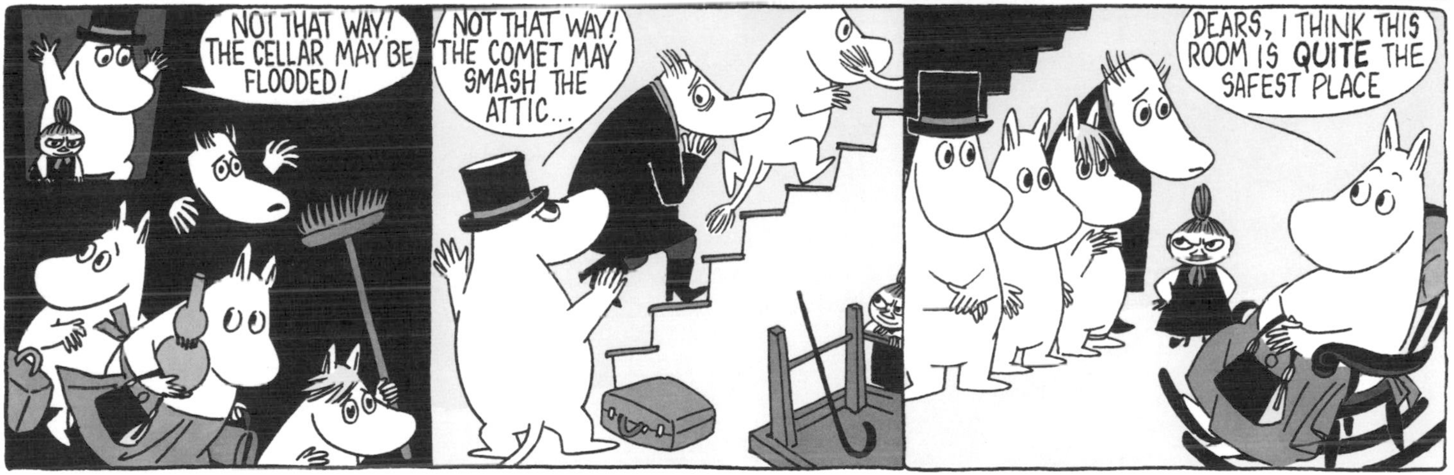
NOT THAT WAY! THE CELLAR MAY BE FLOODED!
NOT THAT WAY! THE COMET MAY SMASH THE ATTIC...
DEARS, I THINK THIS ROOM IS **QUITE** THE SAFEST PLACE

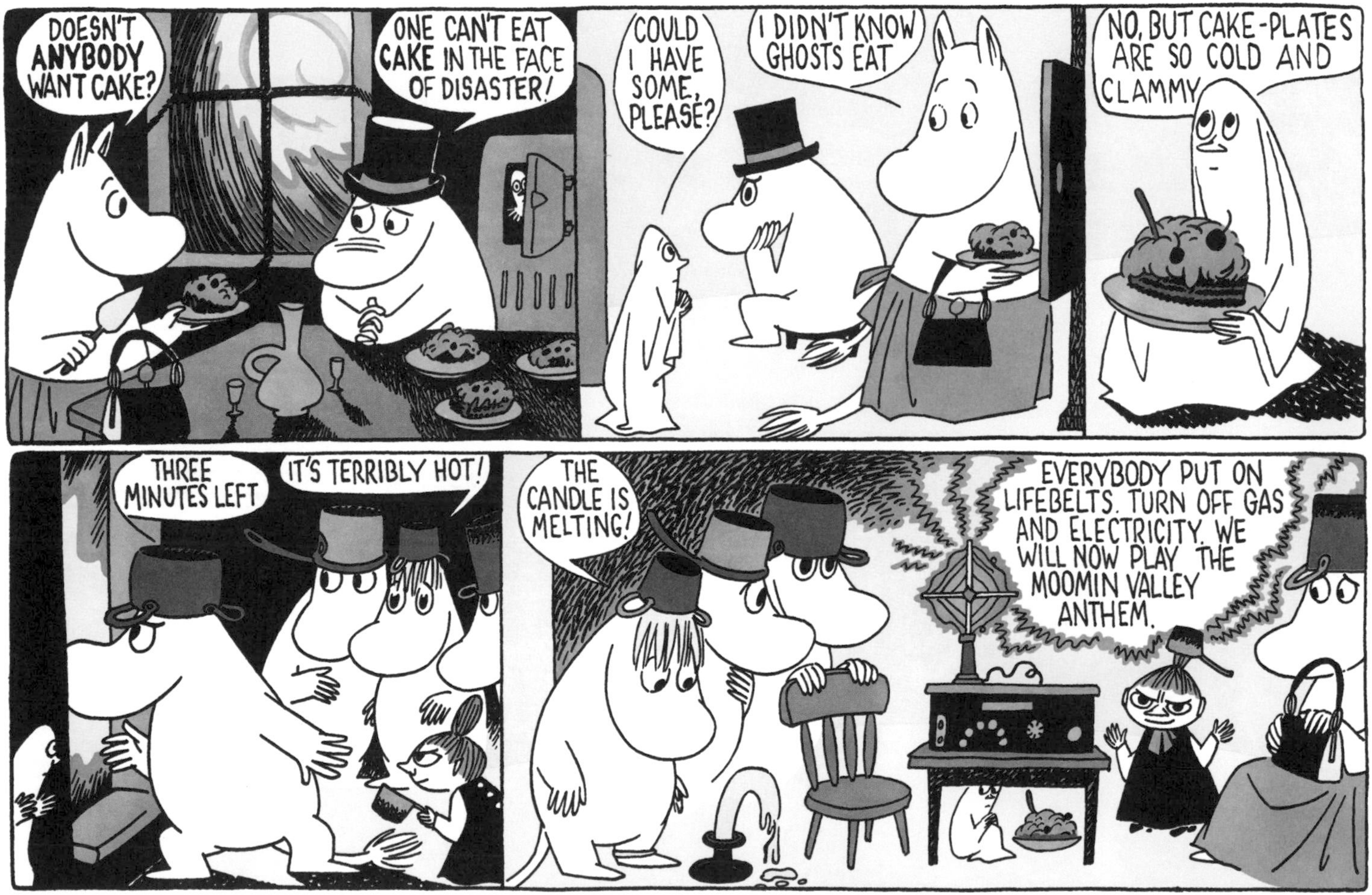
DOESN'T ANYBODY WANT CAKE?
ONE CAN'T EAT CAKE IN THE FACE OF DISASTER!
COULD I HAVE SOME, PLEASE?
I DIDN'T KNOW GHOSTS EAT
NO, BUT CAKE-PLATES ARE SO COLD AND CLAMMY
THREE MINUTES LEFT
IT'S TERRIBLY HOT!
THE CANDLE IS MELTING!
EVERYBODY PUT ON LIFEBELTS. TURN OFF GAS AND ELECTRICITY. WE WILL NOW PLAY THE MOOMIN VALLEY ANTHEM.

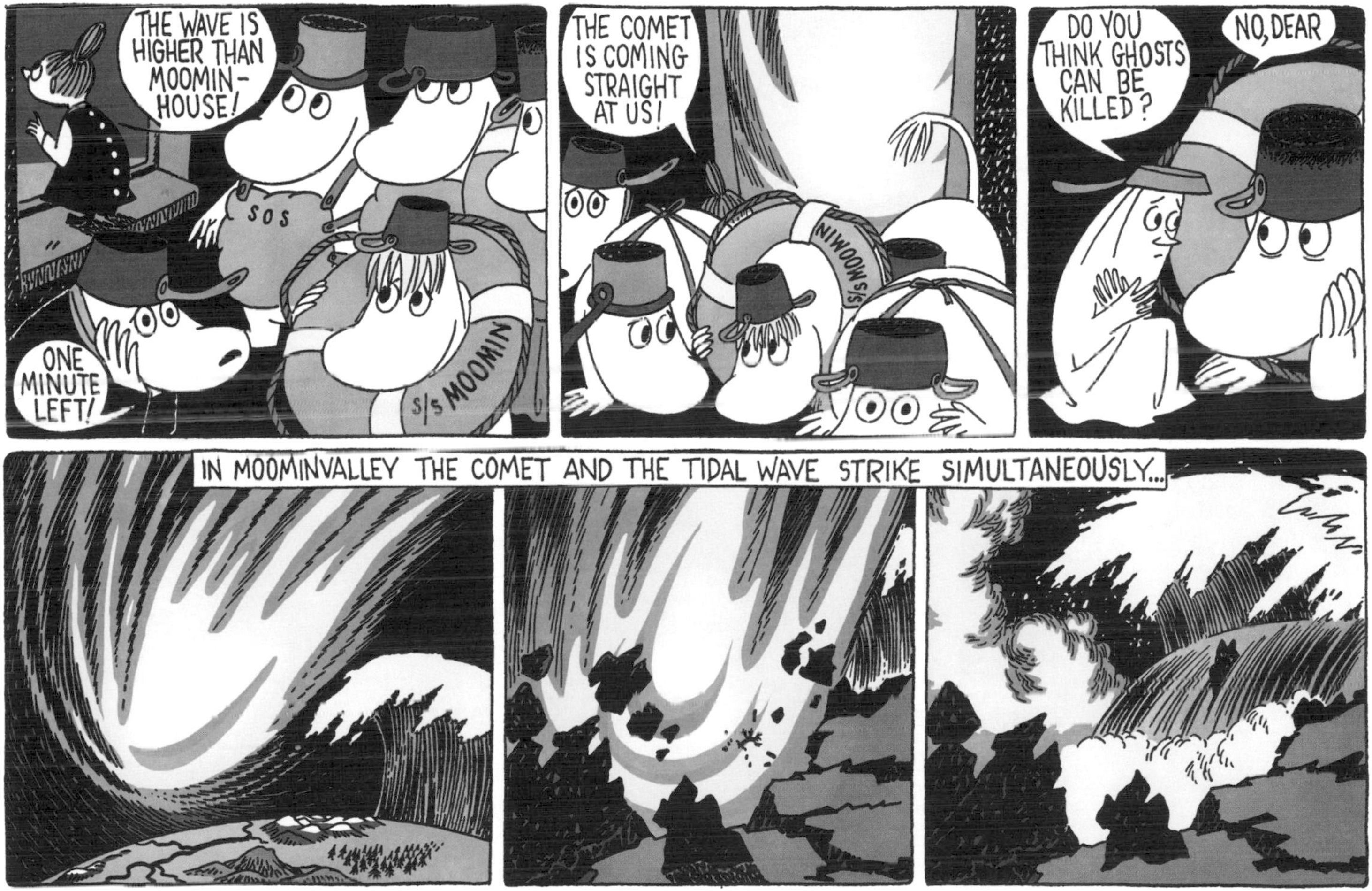
THE WAVE IS HIGHER THAN MOOMIN-HOUSE!
SOS
ONE MINUTE LEFT!
S/S MOOMIN
THE COMET IS COMING STRAIGHT AT US!
S/S MOOMIN
DO YOU THINK GHOSTS CAN BE KILLED?
NO, DEAR
IN MOOMINVALLEY THE COMET AND THE TIDAL WAVE STRIKE SIMULTANEOUSLY...

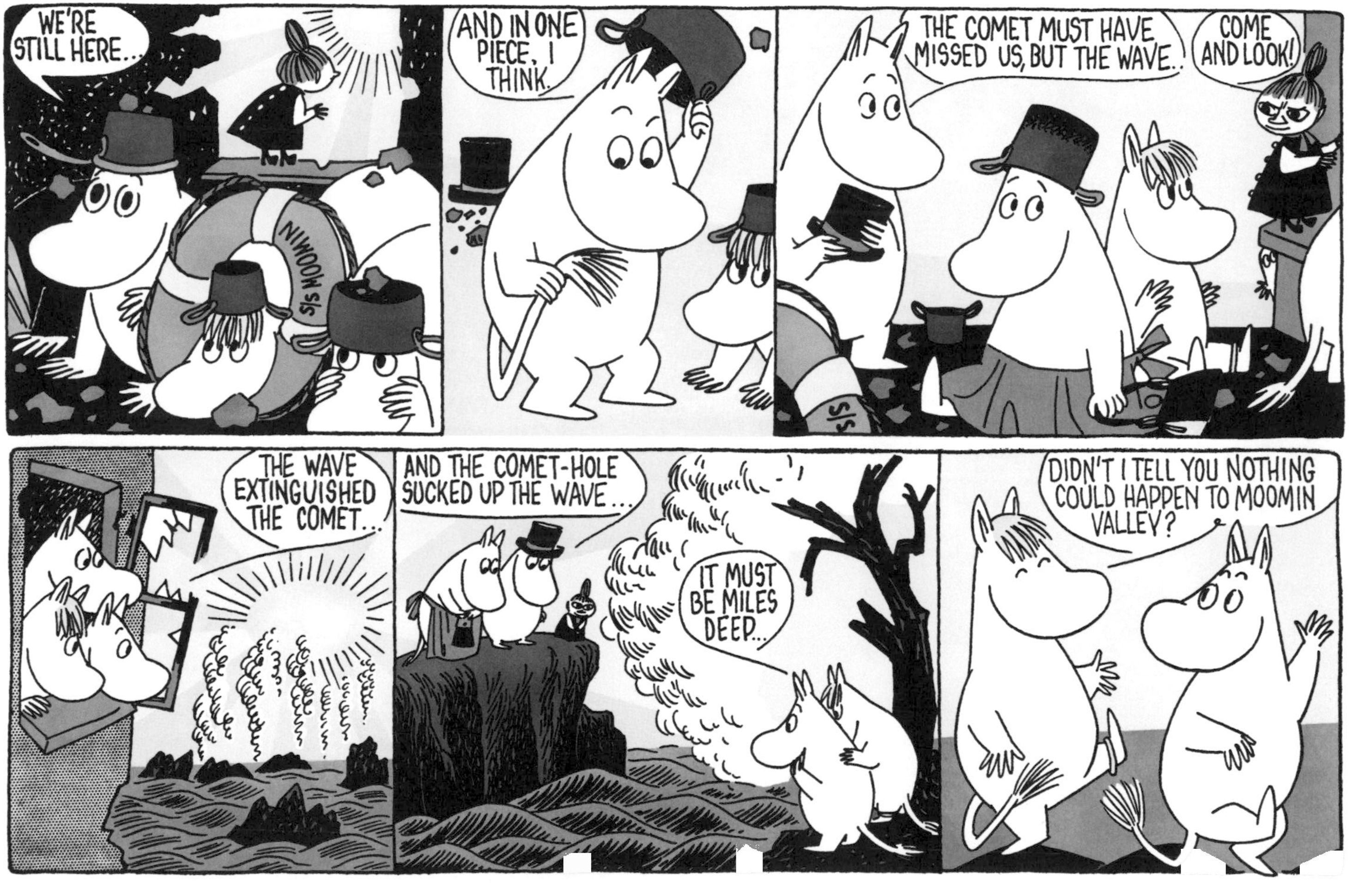
WE'RE STILL HERE...
S/S MOOMIN
AND IN ONE PIECE, I THINK.
THE COMET MUST HAVE MISSED US, BUT THE WAVE..
COME AND LOOK!
S/S
THE WAVE EXTINGUISHED THE COMET...
AND THE COMET-HOLE SUCKED UP THE WAVE...
IT MUST BE MILES DEEP...
DIDN'T I TELL YOU NOTHING COULD HAPPEN TO MOOMIN VALLEY?

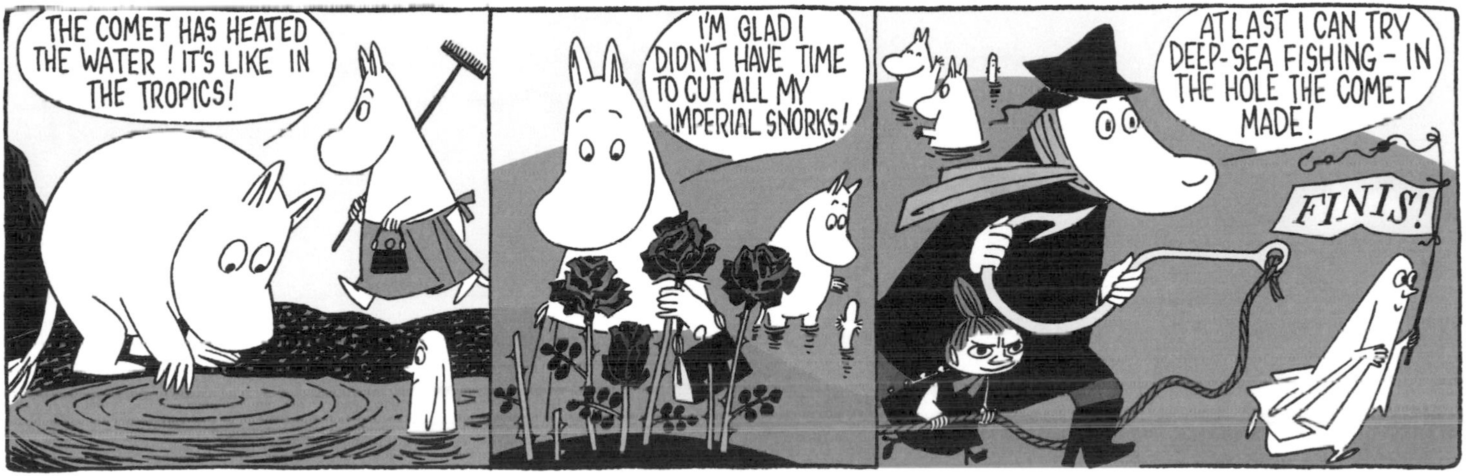
THE COMET HAS HEATED THE WATER ! IT'S LIKE IN THE TROPICS!
I'M GLAD I DIDN'T HAVE TIME TO CUT ALL MY IMPERIAL SNORKS!
AT LAST I CAN TRY DEEP-SEA FISHING – IN THE HOLE THE COMET MADE!
FINIS!

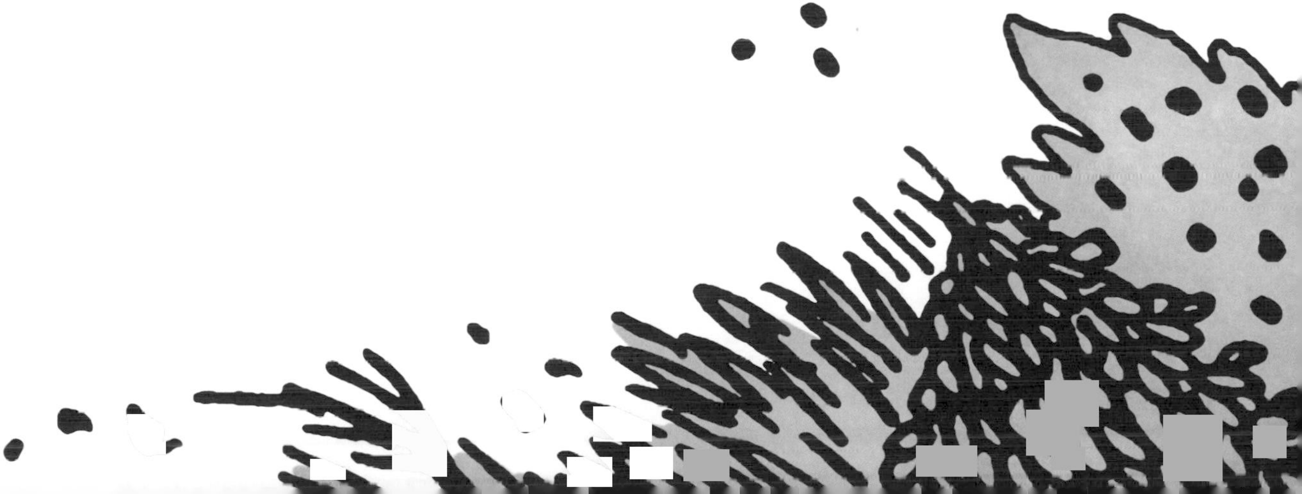

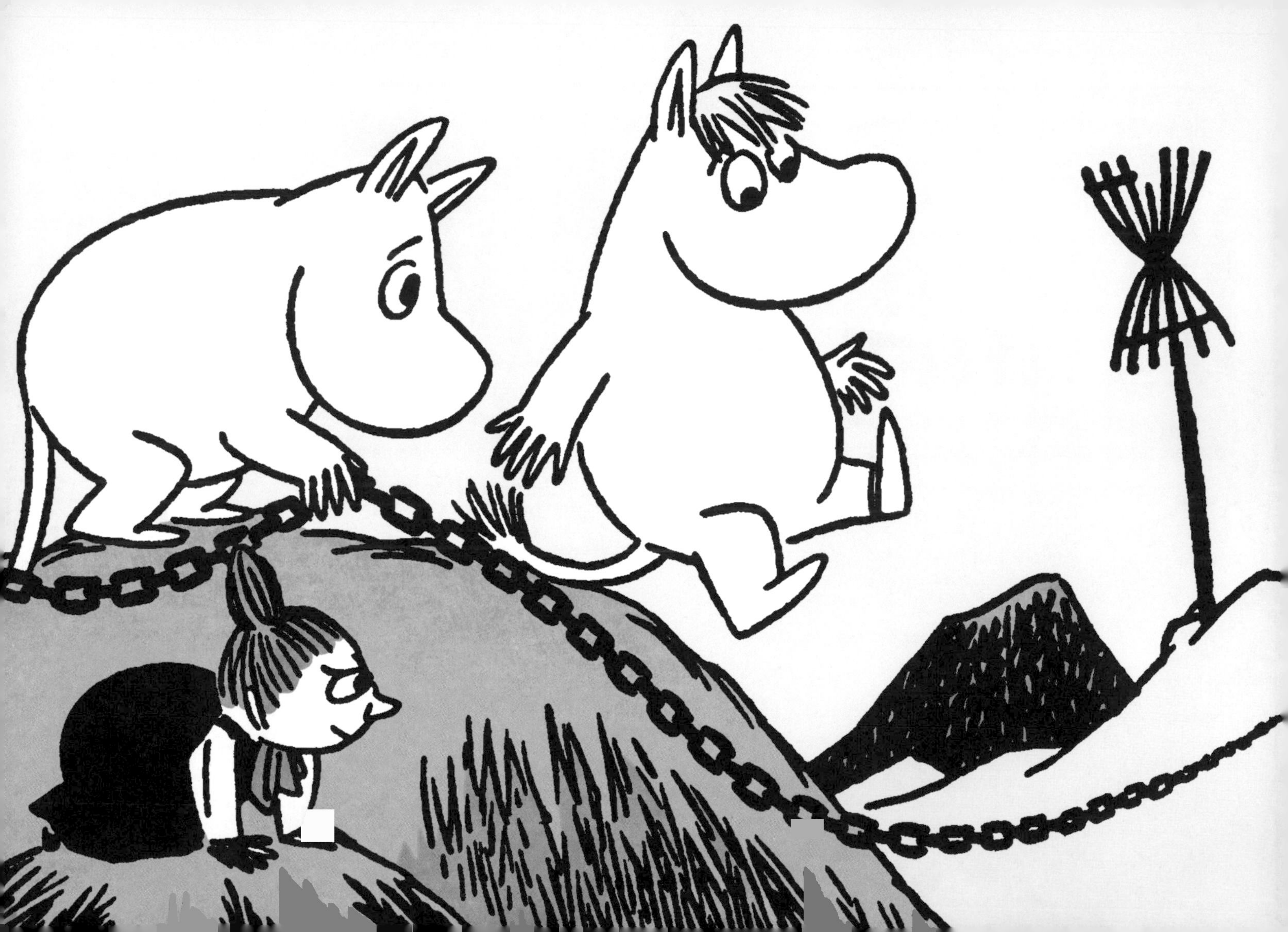

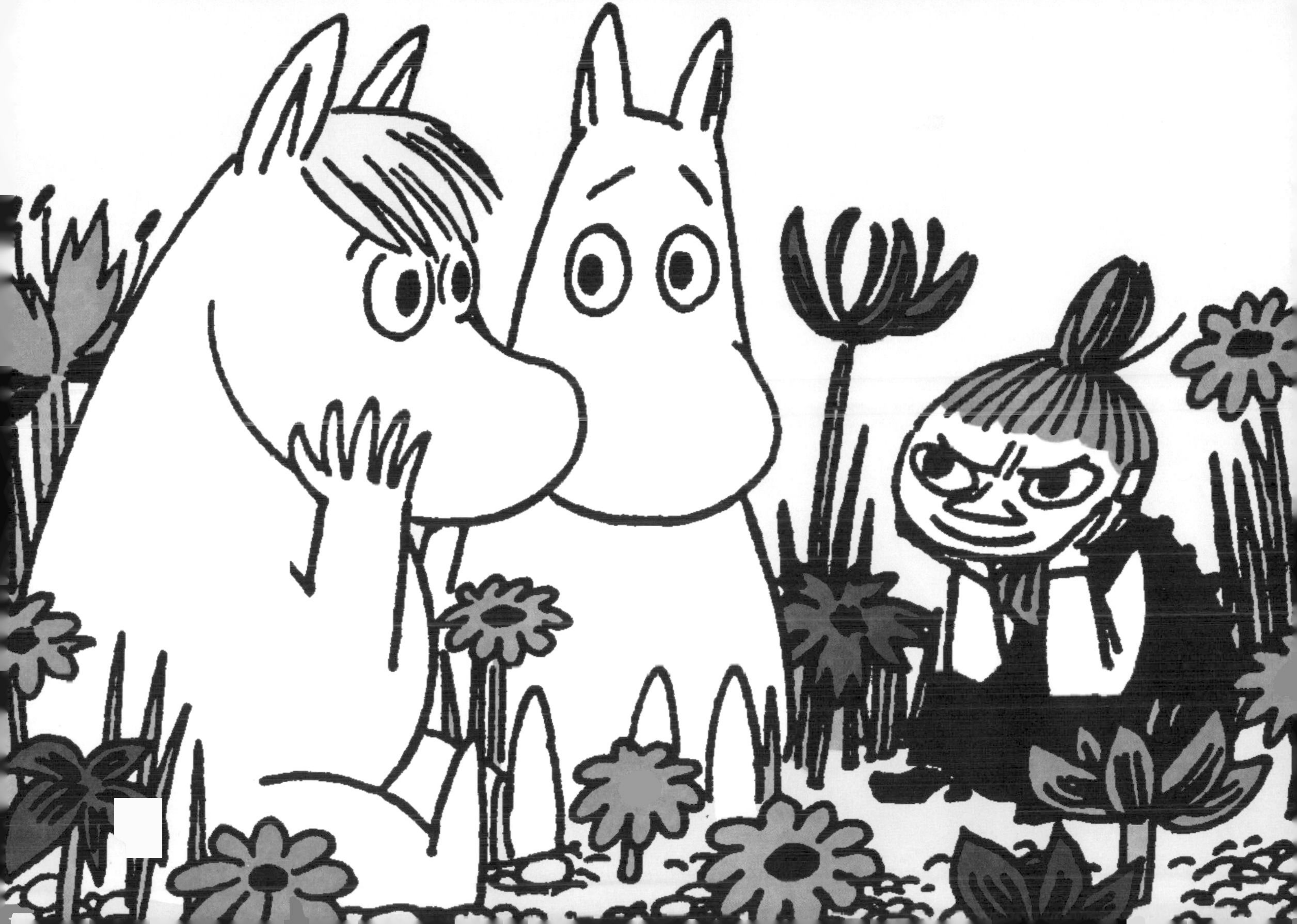

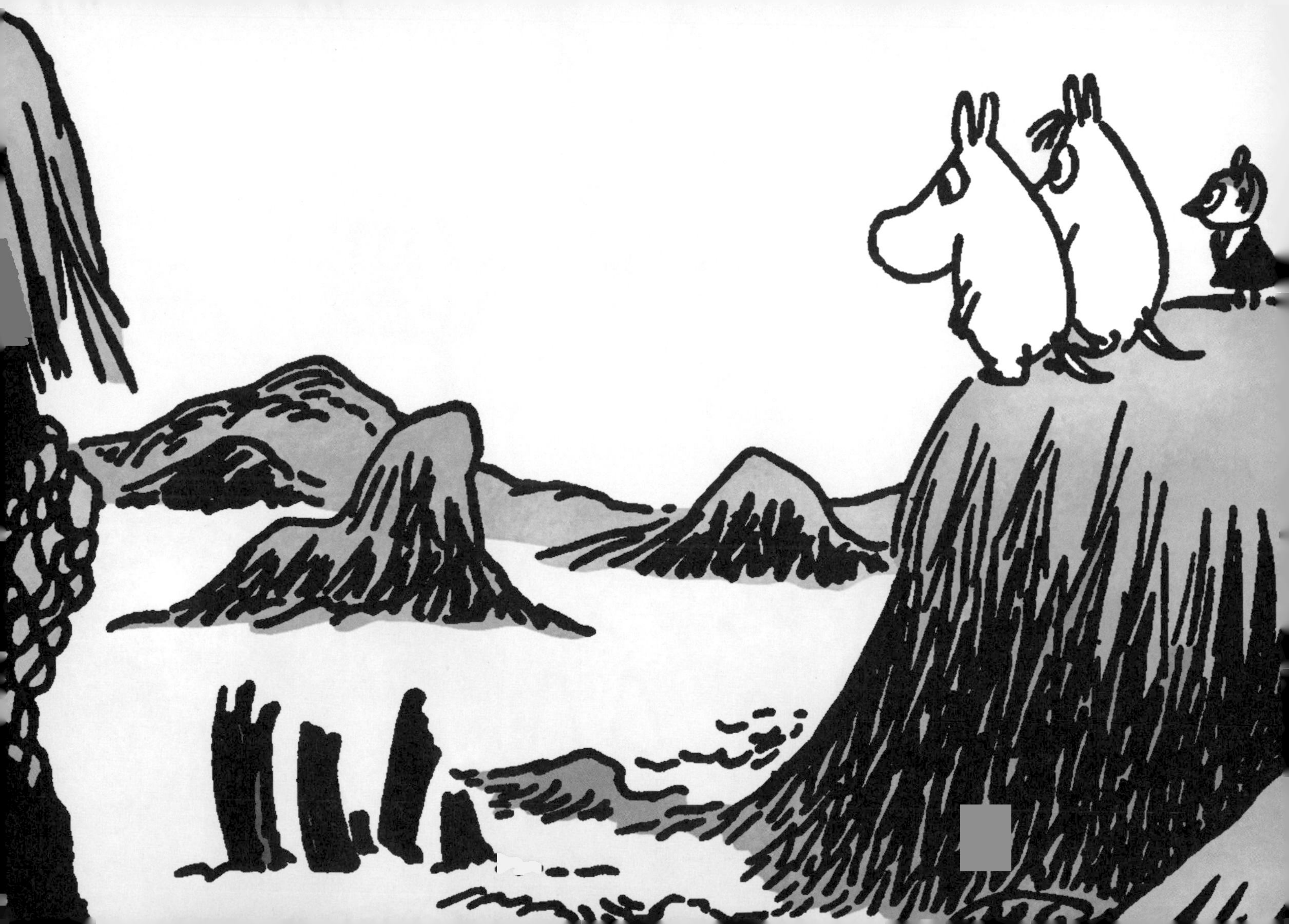

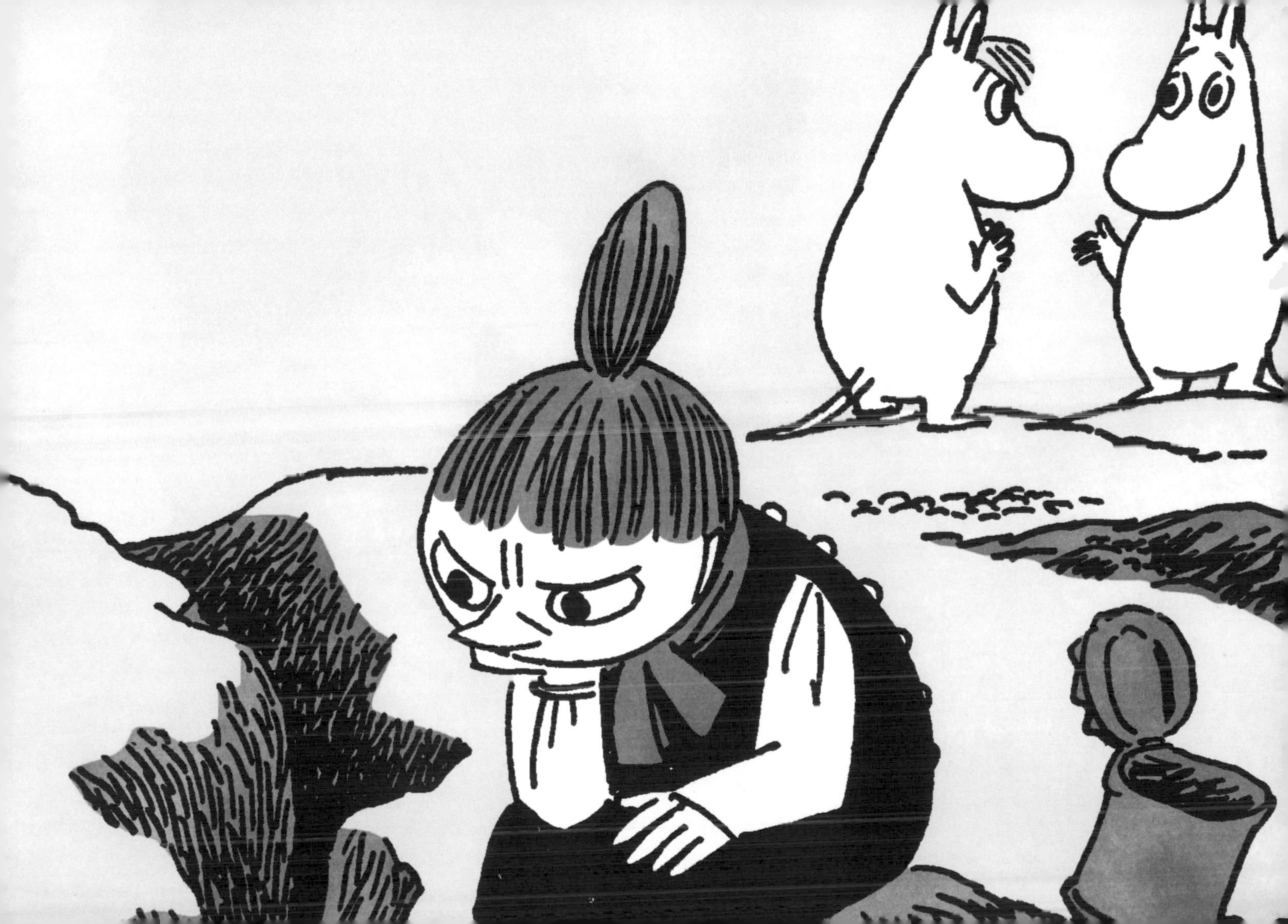

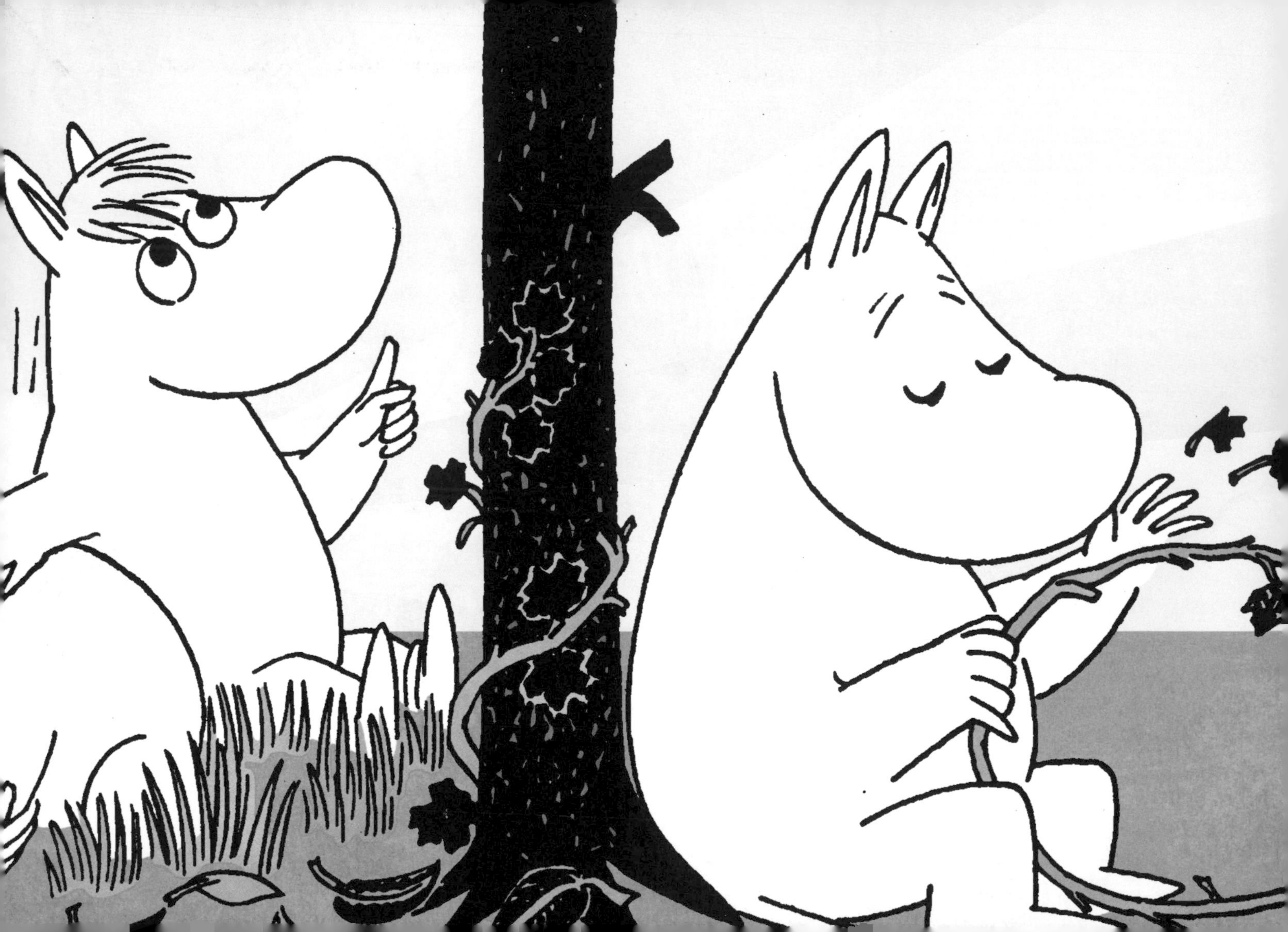